THE

INDESTRUCTIBLE

MACHINES

Taran Richards

The Fabrakkan Chronicles chart the many adventures of a group of children as they visit the ancient machine world of Fabrakka. Time itself on Fabrakka is broken, and with each visit to this mysterious world, the children experience a different Age of Fabrakka - from its Dark Petrification to its New Golden Age, and from the very dawn of the world to its ultimate destruction and rebirth as something entirely new.

Within these adventures, the children meet an incredible array of amiable and eccentric, sentient machines who they befriend and team up with to help restore the world and Time itself. But there is a singular evil arisen in Fabrakka, one that exists outside of Time across all the Ages - an evil that will stop at nothing to take Fabrakka, its powerful treasures, and every machine in it - for itself.

PROLOGUE

A unique world exists, one that touches our own and is filled with wondrous impossibilities. It is a vast land, etched with invisible energy lines, whose intersections whisper to those in our own world, and perhaps many others.

The raw materials of this place are the darkest and blackest of blacks - so devoid of all light that the human eye could not fully appreciate it, and the human brain can barely comprehend it. And yet, every surface in this blackened world shimmers with a translucent, silver energy that creates a restless medley of colour in the skin of all things.

This world is punctuated with extraordinary gleaming cityscapes, bursting with complex interweaving structures and spires that stretch high into the sky and whose tops break through the clouds into yet another realm above. Between these great cities lie immense wildernesses, composed of powerful raw minerals - harder and more densely packed than any substance humans have ever encountered or studied.

In this other world, nothing has ever died, nor has there ever been conflict or any form of hardship. It is a world populated by diverse, good-natured machines; made by machines and run by machines for the good of all machines. All are considered equal and all share the same purpose of building a perfect, unspoilt world.

This goal - they achieved. But that perfect world has been corrupted and lost...

CHAPTER ONE

Three Children and a House

The children stared silently at the mansion from the relative safety of the uneven, weed-covered pavement outside. The large house was in almost total darkness, even though it was only late afternoon and the sun had not yet set. The paint had peeled and faded from its exterior, and with few intact windows remaining to reflect any light, it appeared far gloomier than anything else neighbouring it. There were dark, spiky plants creeping up the outside of the house that the children had never seen before, and they were not overly keen to know what species they were.

'He went mad... so they say,' said Lewis, in a somewhat unconvincing manner.

Kat looked her brother up and down, then rolled her eyes, signalling her disapproval of his all too familiar and forced grown-up tone of voice.

'Who told you that?' she retorted with a sneer as she continued tying up her dark wavy hair, which was generously flecked with long red strands.

'Everyone knows it,' Lewis replied, with a little hesitation. 'Back me up, Artie. The professor went mad - and then just disappeared. Right?'

Artie did not reply, but instead continued staring at the broken house, scratching his head through his tousled, mousy-brown hair. He had a puzzled look on his face, as though (even with such an obviously unsettling sight in front of him), something else that he could not grasp was not quite right with this picture. Eventually he did speak, in a calm but determined voice.

'How do we get in?' he asked, although more to himself than to his best friend and his friend's twin sister. 'The outer fence is the only thing that still seems to be in one piece. I've been looking, and I can't see any holes, or gaps, or signs that anyone has ever tried to get inside. Doesn't that seem odd to you?'

Lewis shrugged his shoulders. He had heard all the rumours at school - everyone at some time or another had boasted of being inside the professor's house after dark. Some had claimed to have seen dead bodies, others had found treasure (which of course they had not touched out of respect for the dead - more likely out of fear of being cursed, Lewis thought), and one older, somewhat dislikeable boy named Lloyd, had even claimed that he had seen the professor's ghost itself. Lewis, however, knew that none of these stories were likely true - no-one in his small village school was remotely brave enough to go inside. But he thought, just maybe, he might be... and Artie certainly would be. Although Lewis was many months younger than Artie, he was now slightly taller than his best friend. He *felt* smaller, however - he had often found it hard to compete with Artie's brash confidence and relentless search for adventure. Lewis steeled himself before replying.

'It is odd,' Lewis replied. 'Very odd... maybe we should take... a closer look?' Kat thought her brother did not sound very convincing in his attempt to appear brave, and his continued wavering voice gave it away.

Lewis and Artie moved along the pavement towards the right-hand side of the house, where the fence turned away from the road into even more darkness - away from the dimness of the grotty streetlight. The boys began to search every chunk of metal for weakness. Kat however, strode off towards the left-hand side, seemingly uninterested in their efforts. It was some time before either of the boys noticed that she had not come along with them.

'Kat!' Artie cried after her. 'Where are you?'

Kat did not reply and had already moved around the far side of the house towards the overgrown rear garden and completely out of sight.

'Artie... look here,' said Lewis and pointed to a single link in the fence at ground level that was thinner and weaker than the rest - and had split. 'Do you think...?'

Artie and Lewis stared intently at the small gap, the cogs in both their brains whirring as they tried to figure out how to make the tiny flaw in the fence large enough for them all to fit through - and without any tools to hand. Lewis wondered if he still had time to go home, raid his father's toolbox, and return before they were all called in for dinner.

'Wotcha!' yelled Kat so loudly that both boys lost their footing and collapsed on top of each other. Lewis groaned, then looked up to see his younger-by-nine-minutes sister staring at him from the wild garden on the other side of the fence.

'How did you get in there?' Artie asked, rubbing the side of his head where his best friend's skull had hit his own.

'Tree,' Kat replied as she took a bite of a juicy green apple. 'Round back. Climbed it. Dropped in. Easy.' *CRUNCH*. 'I'll wait.'

The boys sprung back to their feet, still rubbing their heads, but soon broke into a smile and then a run as they gleefully raced around the house to find the tree. Most boys of Lewis' age would be annoyed by such antics of their sister, but he knew better. His mother was always proudly saying that Kat was wise beyond her years, but somewhat less proudly that she did not seem to be afraid of anything at all in this world.

It was not long before all three were reunited in the unkempt garden of the large and broken mansion, again staring at the darkened building - this time from the relative *lack* of safety of the other side of the fence. Lewis gulped as a wave of fear hit him, but he kept it to himself as he could see that neither Artie nor Kat looked the least bit afraid.

'Should we ring... the doorbell?' Lewis asked, his voice breaking once more. 'You know - just to be sure no-one is home...'

Artie laughed, and Kat gave her brother a wry look.

'You've torn your trousers - again,' Kat said to Artie, pointing. Artie's camouflage cargo pants were very scuffed, frayed and the many pockets were full of holes. The logo on his ill-fitting t-shirt had long since faded, and as usual, the laces of his boots were partly undone. Artie did not notice though - it had been some time since the boots had fitted properly - they were now at least half a size too small and he no longer noticed the discomfort. Despite all that, Artie was a rather confident and handsome, stocky boy.

He shrugged and strode up the ornate, curving but crumbling stone stairs towards the heavy wooden front door.

'I guess not then...' said Lewis to himself as he realised Artie had no intention of ringing the doorbell. Lewis followed on behind, trying to keep his distance but make it look as though he was not becoming more and more afraid. Artie pushed the door, expecting it to be either too heavy to move or, more likely, locked. It was neither and it swung open with ease - as though the house wanted them to come in.

The atmosphere changed as soon as they crossed the threshold. The air was thick and musty, and full of dust that made the children cough. The darkness of the interior stifled the three children's minds - making it hard to think clearly. They felt the tension in the house right through to their bones, and they stood for a few seconds in the half-light until they realised that the tension was not caused simply by the darkness and the lack of fresh air. The house itself was pulsing. Throbbing.

'Can you feel that?' asked Kat. 'It feels as though the floor is moving.'

'Not just moving,' said Lewis. 'Vibrating.'

'It's aliiiiiiive!' exclaimed Artie through a self-satisfied chuckle. The children stood still as his words echoed around the vast interior, bouncing around the walls and up the huge staircase into the even darker upper levels.

After a few more seconds Artie broke free of the small pack and started to explore the hallway. The strange throbbing of the house made his legs feel like jelly as he walked over the creaking wooden floors. Even when he stepped onto the dusty thick rug that covered the central part of the hallway, he could still feel the house's vibrations just as strongly. The walls were covered in a rich and elaborate patterned wallpaper that was very faded and in many places peeling, and on much of the walls hung large portraits of unknown people who all looked very important. The wooden beams running across the ceiling were exposed and of a dark mahogany and it was then that Artie noticed something even stranger.

'Look, you guys. Can you see that - in the cracks and grain of the wood?'

Artie stood pointing at the ceiling until Lewis and Kat walked gingerly over to meet him, their legs like jelly too. The roof was peppered with extremely fine rivers of a bright green substance - gently, rhythmically pulsing but clearly moving across the ceiling - and all heading in the same direction.

'Whoa,' said Lewis. 'What is that? I've never seen any ceiling behave like that before.'

'It looks like it's all moving towards that room up there,' said Kat, taking over pointing duties from Artie.

'Come on, then,' said Artie, eager as ever to delve straight into the unknown, and he began to move up the first few steps of the grand staircase.

Kat and Lewis began to follow him more slowly, taking time to look around at the immense oldness of the house. As Artie and Lewis reached the top step of the staircase and looked down the almost pitch-black hallway, Kat called out from below.

'Isn't this him?' she cried out. She was standing half-way up the staircase looking at a portrait - one much smaller than all the others, and in a far more plain frame. If she had not been so curious about the house, she would most likely have walked right past it without even noticing it was there.

Artie and Lewis both rolled their eyes and began the long descent back down the staircase to where Kat had stopped.

'The professor,' she continued. 'This is him, right?'

They all peered at the small, faded black and white photo which was very much out of place in the surroundings of large coloured paintings by highly accomplished artists. There was a small caption underneath the photo which showed a tall thin man in a white laboratory coat standing centrally and surrounded by much smaller, squatter men all wearing lab coats as well. The tall thin man was holding a plaque with writing on it which was too small and faded to make out. Artie blew on the words of the plaque and ran his finger across it to clear away some of the dust.

'Professor J. B. Alexander and colleagues of the National Institute of Physics, Exploratory Department. November 30, 1922,' he read out.

'1922?' Lewis queried as he looked around the dusty house interior. 'How long has this place been left like this?'

Artie shrugged his shoulders again and started back up the staircase calling down towards the others.

'Who cares? Old people, long gone, doing old-people-type-of-things. Come on, let's explore. I want to see what's in that room.'

Artie reached the top of the staircase and again looked down the dark hallway, which he now realised was being gently lit every few seconds by the slow pulsing glow of whatever the green substance in the floorboards was. He waited until a new pulse appeared and followed its path as it travelled across the floor, each tiny fissure of luminescence winding its way through the grains in the wood towards its destination. It was only then that he noticed the green substance was emitting noise, just barely audible; soothing and breathy sounds as though the air was lightly singing. Artie could swear every molecule of the substance seemed to know exactly where it was heading. Soon, he was standing outside a very plain and slightly small door at the end of the hallway as the green pulses travelled underneath it and into the mysterious room beyond.

He grabbed the door handle and turned it and the door began to give way - but suddenly, as though caught by a gust of wind, the door slammed shut in his face.

'Ow!' he yelled, rubbing his hand which had caught the full force of the handle. He looked around to see Kat and Lewis now approaching him, both equally fascinated by the green substance pulsing in the floorboards as he had been. Artie, his hand smarting, tried the handle again - only to find that the door now appeared to be locked and would not budge.

'That's not fair…' he said whilst kissing and shaking his hand to soothe it. 'It started to open for me… then decided against it!'

'The door decided…?' Kat asked with a highly questioning look etched on her face. 'Don't be silly… here - let me have a go.'

Kat grabbed the handle and turned it and the door opened easily and fully, revealing the room beyond.

'You just have to have the knack,' she grinned, repeating one of her father's favourite phrases. The three children stepped into the room and at the same time all three said the exact same thing.

'Whoooaaa!'

Standing at the far end of the room - a room that looked too big to fit into the space suggested by the plain, petite door and average hallway outside, was an enormous contraption. It was the deepest black colour they had ever seen, but completely smooth and reflective like glass that had been polished until it could not be polished any more. The machine was extraordinary in every way - pipes, and coils and tubes burst forth from every direction - switches, levers, dials, gauges and bulbs adorned many surfaces and almost everything was made of that same blackened glassy material.

The children slowly walked towards the machine and then all around it, taking it in. Lewis peered as closely as possible at the main body of it and on its underside felt a series of protruding symbols that he did not recognise and could not figure out. Kat was trying to understand the impossibly dark yet shiny material that looked utterly without flaw - there were no rivets, seams or joins that she could detect - even all the tubes that connected to its main body seemed to simply grow effortlessly out of it. The entire contraption looked as though it was all one seamless moulded piece. She ran her fingers gently over the switches and dials - making sure not to press too hard for fear of activating something - and tried to understand how something so complex could look so streamlined even with all its pipes and dials. The deep blackness of the machine was not the only thing that she noticed - it had a sense of restlessness about it, as though the outer skin of the machine was moving - very, very slowly but gently swirling like it was made of very thick oil. She could not actually see it move - but she could definitely feel it. Artie, however, stopped after a few seconds and just stared - his brain trying to put the pieces together of the odd sight in this odd room in this rather odd house.

'Look,' he said, finally. 'That green substance is working its way into the machine - see it running across the floorboards and then up its - well, legs I guess.'

'You're right,' said Lewis. 'But then the stream of green stuff just fades out - to nothingness - as though it has nowhere left to go to.'

'How do we switch it on?' asked Artie impatiently, as he scanned the floor and then behind the machine for some sort of cable or plug to attach it to the electricity supply.

'Switch it on!' cried Lewis. 'Are you mad? We have no idea what it is! It could be a bomb!'

'It's not a bomb,' retorted Artie nonchalantly. 'I mean, it doesn't look like any bomb I've ever seen... not on television anyway.'

'Well that hardly qualifies you as an expert does it?' said Lewis, who was about to continue when Kat interrupted.

'Erm... guys,' she said hesitantly and started to point. 'I think something is happening...'

She was right - from one of the dials a white glow began growing brighter and longer until it looked like the sort of light that comes out of a movie projector. The light finished in a thin circle that hung in the air, and gradually got bigger and bigger.

'Look at this...' said Lewis as he moved closer to the beam of light.

Normally, when a light is shone in a dark room, (such as the light from a torch), all the particles that move with the currents of air swirl around in the light as though they are dancing. That was, however, not what Lewis was seeing at all. Instead, all those particles that would usually dance around were simply stuck - hanging frozen within the beam of light. At the edge of the beam of light he saw a small fly - its head was just inside the light, completely still, but its body was outside of the beam and its wings were flapping furiously - but the fly was stuck going nowhere fast.

'Wow,' said Artie as he joined Lewis to look. 'That is super-freaky - and look at this!' he said as he moved back towards the machine.

The machine was also changing - previously, where the green substance faded to nothing as it reached the legs of the machine, it had now started to work its way up and over the darkened glass in thousands of thin fissures that seemed to be embedded deep below its surface - entirely invisible before. The more of the machine that became covered, the bigger the circle of white light became.

Suddenly there was an enormous cracking sound from the ceiling of the room and the three children looked up to see the beams of the roof splinter and rip apart. Another crack appeared in the far wall, followed by another across the floor - the whole room had started to collapse inwards. Kat, Lewis and Artie all yelled and screamed at once as huge chunks of wood, plaster and brick exploded and fell all around them.

'Let's get out of here!' yelled Lewis and they all began to move towards the door they entered the room by. But before they could reach it, the floor between themselves and the door collapsed and, as they regained their balance, (narrowly avoiding falling into the chasm below), the door imploded in a mass of splintered wood and disappeared as though it had been sucked into an invisible vortex.

The three children looked around frantically as parts of the room exploded outwards whilst other sections of the room collapsed in on itself. Soon they found themselves backing away from the chaos surrounding them on all sides, but unaware they were backing towards the growing circle of white light which was now spinning furiously.

Kat looked down at her feet to see that only a few floorboards and beams remained for them to stand on - then she looked up to see that almost nothing of the room, and in fact the entire house, was visible anymore and she found herself staring at mostly blackness.

'What's happening?' she yelled.

The last thing she saw and heard was the machine detonating in a bright green explosion that completely enveloped her and took her breath away.

CHAPTER TWO

Air, Dirt and Water

Lewis tried to open his eyes and immediately began to panic. He clutched at his throat and gasped and felt so dizzy he thought he was going to be sick.

'Breathe,' came a soothing voice. 'Just breathe.'

It was so dark he could not make out who was talking - his ears felt blocked as though he was underwater, and the voice was very muffled.

'Can't... breathe,' he panted. 'No... air!'

'There is air,' came the voice. 'Take a deep breath... just relax.'

Lewis nodded his head in understanding and took a deep breath as instructed. A small amount of light started to make its way into both his blue left eye and his grey right eye, and as the total darkness started to fade, he began to make out fuzzy shapes that slowly became sharper. He sighed relief as he realised that he could, sort of, breathe - although it was difficult.

'I felt the same when I first woke up... but it passes after you take... a few breaths,' said Artie. 'It's like the air isn't... the same as we are used to. There must be some oxygen in it... or we'd all be dead by now I'm sure... but maybe the mixture... is different. It tastes a little weird anyway.'

Lewis slowly began to sit upright. He shook and gently banged his head with his hands as though trying to dislodge some water from his ears that was not there. He smoothed out his fair hair, and began to dust down his neat, well-fitted jeans, t-shirt, cardigan and shoes - he hated the idea of being dirty - but he soon realised that there was actually no dust or debris to remove.

'Thank you... Professor Artie,' he said, grimacing and tightening his shoelaces, then suddenly felt a wave of panic as he remembered what had happened. 'Kat!' he yelled.

'I'm here,' she responded from nearby. 'I'm fine... just a little... woozy like you.' She panted a little as she spoke. 'Have you noticed...' she began, '...how stale the air is? Like it's... not moving? Where are... we anyway?'

'I know...' responded Artie, '...and it's neither cold nor warm. It's almost like we just can't feel anything at all.'

The three children looked around as their eyes collectively, finally cleared. They appeared to be outdoors - they could not see any walls or ceiling anyway, but neither could they see very much in the near-darkness. Lewis, who was still sitting on the ground, ran his hands over the ground beneath him.

'It's not a bomb...' he muttered under his breath sarcastically as he grabbed what he assumed was a handful of dirt. He tried to let it slip through his fingers, but it fell so very, very slowly and seemed to take an age to reach the ground again even though he had only lifted it a couple of centimetres.

'What *is* this - it feels odd?' he said. 'Not dirty like dirt normally does - but both sharp and smooth at the same time - like tiny shards of glass that have had all the roughness removed. I can't really explain it - it feels very wrong.'

It was then that he saw the dirt was pulsing in the same way that the green substance in the house had - only this time it was glowing red, crackling and hissing rather than pulsing and singing, and behaving in a much more erratic way than the rhythmic and predictable green substance had been. Across the ground, tiny fissures ran in thousands of different directions, illuminating the area immediately around them. The ground looked as though it had been invaded and infected by the redness. They could finally see that they were most certainly outside, and it seemed to be getting very gradually lighter as though the sun was coming up - but there was no obvious direction the cold light was coming from - it seemed to be coming from every direction all at once.

'I don't think it is actually getting lighter,' began Artie. 'I think our eyes are just adjusting to the darkness. Have you noticed how still everything is? I haven't heard any kind of sound at all. Except us. No birds, or insects. Not even the rustle of branches - and there's no breeze - I guess that partly explains why the air tastes so odd. I'm not sure anything actually lives here.'

Lewis got to his feet and then helped Kat to hers. Artie, who was crouched on his haunches, stood upright and moved closer to the other two.

'What now?' he asked, looking around. 'Are we still inside the house, but in some weird other place within it? Are we inside that big wobbly white-light circle thing? Have we been shrunk to tiny insect size and everything just looks and feels different because we're so very small?' As he rambled his way through the possibilities, he became more and more excited and a smile spread across his face.

'This is so cool!' he exclaimed.

It was just then that Kat's face flushed red and screwed up as though she was trying to stop herself from crying. As her face reddened, the light dusting of freckles across her cheeks and nose became prominent - standing out even more against the beige cable-knit sweater that she practically lived in. Lewis noticed immediately and put his arm around his sister while Artie obliviously carried on spouting more and more elaborate scenarios. It was the first time (since she was very young) that Lewis had seen his sister even slightly afraid or upset.

'Shut up!' Lewis yelled. 'How do we get home?'

Artie stopped mid-sentence as he realised not everyone was as thrilled as he was to be in another dimension, or on another planet or wherever it was the exploding machine had catapulted them to. Artie loved science at school; his teachers had said he had a natural aptitude for all the sciences - and the chance to make new discoveries had overwhelmed him.

'Oh,' he said as his eyes also filled a little with water. 'I'm sorry. Home. Yes. Home. Good plan.' Artie stopped and stared at his distressed friends in silence as he finally realised how scary the situation truly was. Just then, something happened.

'CHILDREN!' boomed a voice.

The three children, now *all* startled and afraid, looked frantically around to see where the voice had come from - but they could not see anything nearby except a small hill that was more obvious to their adjusted eyes than it had been before. Artie took a few steps towards the hill before Kat called out.

'Don't!' she said, and Artie slowed. He looked back at the two of them, but then carried on walking - albeit more cautiously now. 'Be careful, then,' urged Kat as she realised that she would not be able to talk him out of exploring.

Artie peered round the side of the hill that, like everything else they could see, was made of the same glowing red and impossible sharp-smooth-blackened-glass-dirt. Nothing could have prepared him for what he saw there.

A rather rotund machine was partly sunk into the ground - its thick legs were covered by the odd dirt and had what appeared to be arms sticking out either side, although at the end were large clamps rather than fingers. It had an extra section near the top that sort of looked like a head - but this was not at the top of any kind of neck; rather the head and face-plate were positioned just slightly above its chest. Beneath its chest there was a large protrusion that Artie thought closely resembled Lewis' father's growing beerbelly. The machine had three dials on its face-plate that sort of looked like eyes - but these were arranged in a neat triangle. As Artie looked closer he could see that all three dials were slightly different; one looked like some kind of lens, one like a type of pressure gauge and the third more closely resembled a compass. Artie doubted those were the dials' actual functions as they did not look quite right, and before he could figure out what they were for, he was distracted by the machine's bulky arms that were now waggling around as though it was trying to free itself from the dirt-trap. The strange hunchbacked machine was made of the same highly polished blackened-glass material that the machine in the mansion-room was, and despite being so bulky and thick-set, the seam-free blackness gave it a very sleek and elegant appearance that also appeared to be moulded from one continuous piece. To Artie's eyes, this new contraption was a mass of contradictions.

'Ah,' it said. 'Perhaps you could render some assistance…'

Artie looked the odd machine up and down and quickly decided that it looked friendly enough. Besides, he thought - even if it was not friendly, it was the one that was trapped. He peered round the dirt mound and gestured to Kat and Lewis to come to him, which they did - with very puzzled looks on their faces. When Kat saw the machine wriggling around in the glowing red dirt, she could not help but smile and suddenly felt a whole lot better.

'Grab an arm,' Artie instructed - Lewis took hold of the machine's left arm clamp while Artie grabbed the right. As he did so, Artie noticed that the machine had the same tiny fissures of the glowing green substance running across it, but far less and much paler than they had seen before - as though there was not much of the green substance to go around.

'One…two…three!' counted Artie and then they pulled.

The hulking machine came free rather easily - much to the surprise of all the children, although there was a lot of thin steam and hissing that escaped from the virtually invisible connections around its leg joints. It seemed rather unstable on its feet - it stumbled around for a short while, until its large feet finally planted firmly on the ground, and it used its odd-looking arms to balance itself. Kat wondered why a machine of that bulky stature could not have freed itself from such a weak and shallow dirt-trap. The machine was slightly taller than both Kat and Artie, but was slightly shorter than the gangly, thin, lanky Lewis.

'My situation has been significantly enhanced,' it said. 'I bestow upon you my hearty felicitations and gratitude.'

'What did it say?' asked Kat.

'I think…' said Artie, '…that it's saying hello and thanks.' Turning to the machine he then said, 'Wherever did you learn to talk?'

The machine made a similar noise that some grownups do when they try to clear their throats, which was odd because it had no obvious throat or even an obvious mouth when it was not talking.

'Children, I have been monitoring and analysing your linguistic exchanges and have extrapolated and refactored my communications database to include your specific verbal vernacular.'

'What?' said Kat again.

'I think…' said Artie, '…it's saying that it has been listening to us and has now figured out how to speak to us in our own language. I guess it has some sort of dictionary or translator inside it.'

'Oh,' said Kat, feeling a little less comfortable at the thought she had been spied on.

'Do you have a name?' asked Lewis, '…and, how did you get stuck… and what is this place… and how did we get here?'

The needles in two of the machine's dials-for-eyes bounced back and forth and spun rapidly as it rotated its head section to face Lewis; then all three dials rotated so that the lens-like one was at the top, and it stuck out a little as it focused in on Lewis.

'I was assigned the designation, that in your language, reads 8L-45-TR by my Maker, and I have been stuck for... well, I am not sure how long. There was nothing, then there was a large flash of green light and then I awoke. I heard your voices but did not have enough power to see or to free myself. Slowly though, I could feel power returning to my machinery and once my boot programme had fully completed - I called out to you. As for how you arrived here - I do not have that information in my current programme. Now, may I ask - what species are you?'

'Why,' said Kat, rather taken aback by the question. 'We're humans.'

'From Earth,' offered Artie, hoping that might mean something to the machine.

'Humans,' mused 8L-45-TR. 'I am unaware of this species. My sensory apparatus detects that you appear to be some sort of biological construct. How very curious. In which facility were you grown?'

The children all laughed at the strange question.

'We were born, not constructed,' said Lewis, '...but I guess after that we did grow. We still are growing. That's what children do.'

'Fascinating,' said 8L-45-TR. 'And did your Makers give you individual designations or do you share a master designation between you all?'

'I'm Lewis,' said Lewis. 'This is my sister Kat, and my friend Artie.' The children each gave the machine a short, reserved wave as though they were officially saying hello for the first time.

'8L-45-TR...' pondered Artie. 'That's a mouthful. I don't think we can keep calling you that. Why don't we just call you Eight?'

The dials in Eight's 'eyes' began moving erratically, and its head section began spinning back and forth inside its housing. All kinds of clunking and whirring sounds sprang forth from its innards in what seemed to Kat to be a very displeased manner. She wondered how the machine could look so sleek and seamless on the outside but sound like a hundred busy old factories on the inside.

'I am 8L-45-TR, sole On-Demand-Detonation-Mining-Unit of the world of Fabrakka!' it said with what appeared to be indignation. After a few seconds, however, its eyes and head calmed and the clunking and the banging noises from its innards faded away. 'But you can call me Eight if you like,' it said through a mechanised sigh.

Kat stepped forward and gently laid her right hand on Eight as if to say *there-there*. Suddenly the surface of Eight's entire machine-body was awash with the green substance that spread rapidly over it. Again, Eight's dials and head section went haywire and inside it whirring noises sprang forth much louder than before. This time though, the noises sounded more like when a brand new and powerful car engine is revved, and much less like when a washing machine starts to break down.

'Whooo-ooo-aaa-aaa!' yelled Eight as it seemed to lose all control. After a few seconds, the spinning slowed, the noises once again faded and Eight seemed to return to normal - whatever normal was for this curious contraption.

'You have the power of this world inside you!' Eight bellowed in sheer delight. 'How is this possible? And... and... what is this?' it continued, as its dials bounced back and forth in much the same way people's eyes do when they are searching inside their brain for a long-lost thought or memory. 'A new database has been incorporated into my systems. Let me see... *Wotcha*? What is this collection of data?'

Lewis, Artie and Kat all stared at one another and gestured with a collective shrug of their shoulders. Kat looked down at her fingers to see that they were pulsing and sparking with the same green substance, before slowly fading away. The sensation she felt in the tips of her fingers was a very pleasant one - a little like being gently tickled.

'What do you mean?' asked Lewis.

'Ah...' began Eight as it continued to think deeply. 'There is much about your situation and my own situation that we must resolve before we can understand these strange occurrences. Perhaps I should first recount the tale of what has happened to my world. That may help us collectively extrapolate how one of you has come to have such extraordinary and unique powers. You biological beings should probably make your fleshy containers comfortable.'

'What?' said Kat yet again, growing more frustrated by Eight's strange use of their language.

'We should sit down while he gives us a history lesson,' said Artie. 'Sounds like it could be a long one...'

It was just then that Artie's stomach rumbled.

'Oh!' exclaimed Artie. 'In all the excitement we forgot just what a pickle we're in. There doesn't appear to be any food or water around here. What are we going to do?'

Kat and Lewis looked at him and realised just how scary it was to be stranded somewhere unknown without anything to eat or drink.

'What is food and water?' asked Eight. 'Why do you require it?'

'Food gives us energy,' replied Artie. 'We need it to be able to move and think. We need water most of all - without water we will die rather quickly.'

'Hmmm...' said Eight, pondering. 'I do not yet know this word - *die*. But water I think I may know. We machines require various liquids to lubricate and cool our internal mechanisms. We produce what I think you mean by water as a simple by-product of our functions. We usually discard it and let it naturally evaporate - but you humans consume it to help you function? You are very strange creatures indeed... but this I can help you with.'

Artie, Kat and Lewis watched as Eight began to shudder, whirr and clunk inside - and after a few more seconds, they could hear bubbling and sloshing too. From nowhere, a small join appeared and grew - and then a flap opened with a gentle click and a thin platform was pushed out. On it, there were three perfectly formed (and rather large) droplets of what appeared to be crystal clear, cold water. The droplets held their shape perfectly without spilling or overflowing at all.

The three children looked at one another with delight, then Artie generously gestured to Kat to take the first drink, which she did, gladly. She pinched the droplet between her fingers and deposited it carefully into the palm of her hand, which was a very strange sensation as she expected it to burst and flood everywhere at any second. It held together without any problem though, and once they had each drank their droplet and were suitably refreshed, Eight continued to speak.

'We will address the issue of food soon enough,' the machine said. 'Now, whilst Time is not working against us, I shall tell you how the world of Fabrakka - for that is where you are - came to be this way…'

CHAPTER THREE

The Indestructible Machines

Many stories begin with 'Once Upon A Time…' or 'A Long Time Ago…' but Eight began its tale with the more unusual:

'The past is somewhat unclear. I do not know all that happened, but I can recount what I know of this world and all that I observed in the final moments as our world began to slow.'

'For many, many cycles - two thousand five hundred and sixty-seven to be precise - we lived in complete peace. All machines worked together harmoniously with the sole purpose of constructing a bigger, better and more efficiently run world. No machine ever wanted for any critical component or source of power and we took great care to build the facilities we desired without compromising the integrity of the natural world or its abundant mineral resources.'

'We are perhaps a unique species, in that we have, by design, ancestral memory. I carry within my memory banks the chipset of my Maker, and its Maker before them, and theirs before them. It is a rite of passage that once a machine decides it has served its purpose in this world as best as it can, that we reuse their physical parts to help build the next required structure or facility or mechanism in our world. We remove their chipset and integrate it into our own systems. As such, no machine has ever perished in this world - what I believe you may have meant when you used the word *'die'* - and even though there may only be a few thousand machines in physical form active at any one time -

there are millions upon millions of minds silently at work. I hope one day to become a Maker - to construct a new machine myself and then, when the time is right, to join with it by passing on my chipset and those of my Maker's lineage. With every iteration of our line we refine and perfect our design, functions and efficiency - for each archetypal machine there is an end goal of true perfection. I myself am approaching the very perfection that my ancestors set out to create all those cycles ago.'

The three children exchanged a look that wordlessly communicated the same thought - that this amiable machine who needed the assistance of small, fleshy beings to help it escape a dirt-trap barely fifty centimetres deep was an odd example of perfection. Eight did not notice (or understand) the look they exchanged and so carried on talking regardless.

'You have seen for yourselves that our world is made from powerful materials. This ground that you sit on is the raw material we call Tekktate - although it is also known by other names as it can be (through a series of complex processes), manipulated into different forms; many of my own components are made largely from it. It is the toughest material we have discovered on this world - it cannot be damaged or broken by any other material or any applied force. But it can be made to be pliable - able to be moulded and reshaped - and once compressed, hardened and polished - is completely indestructible.'

'Hold on,' said Artie. 'Let me see if I have this straight. You're saying that your race of machines cannot be damaged or destroyed and effectively lives forever? And that the structures you have made - not that we have seen any yet - are made from the bones of your parents and grandparents?'

Eight's sleek exterior betrayed the nature of its hidden internal workings, which now whirred and clunked and pinged as it tried to sort Artie's words into the words and meanings it had so far learned or reasoned from its conversations with the children, or from the strange physical contact with Kat.

'Yes,' Eight replied. 'A distasteful manner for describing our existence perhaps, but essentially your description is accurate.'

Kat pulled a face but said nothing. Lewis looked uncomfortable - unsure if it was solely the weirdness of Eight's tale or the ache of sitting on raw Tekktate - or perhaps both. Eight scanned the children, who were now all exhibiting what it thought was rather odd behaviour, before continuing.

'That is how the world was and we had every reason to believe it would always be that way - but then, somewhere in a facility that was unknown to us - hidden from us... v0-LT-2 was constructed.'

The children sat up rigidly at the mere mention of this name. Lewis did not know why, but he suddenly felt more anxious, and as though he was being watched closely by something very far away - a feeling that deepened and that he could not shake, as Eight continued its tale.

'Within just a few short cycles learning of v0-LT-2's existence, our world was forever changed. It is now clear to me that the substance coursing through you, Kat, was the main positive power of our world. We refer to it as Kora, although it was far less concentrated and was silver-white in colour. It flowed through and across everything and provided the constant charge we machines require to function. It powered not just us, but every facility and structure and mechanism in the world. Abundant and safe, we never had any reason to believe that our reliance on it could be exploited negatively. This is where my direct and exact knowledge of events begins to break down. I know that v0-LT-2 managed to take control of one of our central facilities, and I know that it managed to invade our systems. How - I do not know. Why - I do not know. What I do know is that the world's source of power was corrupted, and seas of red washed over everything. This red Kora charge drained our facilities and all machines. Bit by bit we ceased to function - I myself slowed until I could no longer move, could no longer think, and before I could determine a solution to my predicament - I found myself stuck here. Even the great whirring of our facilities ground to a halt and the world no longer turned and fell completely silent... and, as I believe you may have seen with your own dials, Time itself has become stuck, as though something has jammed its very workings. Until Kat touched my outer shell, I had no knowledge of this concentrated, new green form of Kora - perhaps it is the key with which we can unstick Time and restore the world.

'Oh!' cried Lewis as he suddenly realised why the world behaved and felt and even tasted so odd and stale. 'But... if the mechanisms that control Time have become stuck, how can we four move and talk and even breathe? Shouldn't we be stuck as well?'

'It is mere speculation...' responded Eight, '...and I am not one for such inaccurate methodologies. But the means you used to travel to this world may have made you immune from its effects. Perhaps now is the time where you must recount your tale to me as I have done for you.'

The children, sometimes talking over one another, and sometimes including parts of the tale that were not all that important, relayed the events of their entire day to Eight, who remained silent and motionless throughout as though it was not only listening but also formulating a thousand possibilities at the same time. When they had finished, Eight once again spoke.

'This machine you speak of...' it said, '...is very strange. It may be your childlike inaccuracy in describing it, but it seems to be a machine of *this* world - but inside *your* world. Something about it does not quite fit - I cannot reconcile the machines of Fabrakka deliberately manufacturing such a device - although my information on v0-LT-2 is highly limited. Curious. Concerning.'

'However, it seems clear to me that the explosion that took you from your world to this world has imbued all of you with the green Kora - you most of all, Kat. Perhaps you were simply closest to the machine when it detonated, or perhaps it had the ability to choose you. Whilst this green power runs through your fleshy containers, I do not believe the effects of Time will affect you. This explosion of green Kora that brought you here has, it appears, awoken me - and now that Kat has imbued me with significantly more green Kora via her hands, I appear immune also. A word of caution though - we are surrounded by the red Kora in every direction. It will be impossible for us to travel from this place without feeling the effects. Time may behave strangely in areas where the red charge is most dense, and the protection of the green charge insufficient - and it will surely again drain my power. How far we may go is impossible to gauge and how it will affect you fleshy beings is also unknown. We must be cautious where we step and mindful of the risks - for travel to the great city we must if we are to fix the world!'

'Fix the world?' cried Lewis. 'Erm... what about getting us home?'

Eight slowly spun its sleek head all the way round, then spoke glumly to the children.

'There is no manner I can detect near here to return you to your home,' responded Eight. 'In the great city, however, there may be - if we can restart the world. It may require the construction of a new device, which could take some time, but with millions of our minds active again a solution could perhaps be reached. Tell me children, how long does your species generally live for?'

Artie was startled by the question but quickly replied. '70, maybe 80 years - if we're lucky.'

'Ah,' responded Eight as it whirred and clunked once more, converting Earth years into Fabrakkan cycles and back again. 'My hope was that your answer would be closer to five or six hundred. This may be more difficult than I first thought.'

'How far is this city?' asked Artie as he squinted towards the horizon, unable to see any form of structure anywhere.

'It is approximately 9,000 clicks from here,' Eight said as it noticed the confused and worried look on the children's faces. 'Ah...' it continued as its innards whirred and clicked again, '...300 kilometres - to use measurements with which you may be more familiar. Such a distance would normally be trivial - our world has many forms of transportation devices - but without Time or positive power they do not function, of course. Although, this area is somewhat of a wilderness - there is not much here at all. Now, based on my observations of your fleshy containers and the length of your lower appendages, I calculate that you can travel at a maximum of five kilometres per hour; at that constant pace, it would take 60 hours to reach the city limits. I myself prefer to travel by detonation as it is much quicker and requires much less effort - but I do not think your weak flesh containers would withstand the blasts. No matter, let us begin our journey, shall we?'

'Hold on!' said Artie. '60 hours? Without sleep or breaks... or food? We can't manage that!'

'Food, yes - of course,' continued Eight. 'That must be addressed. Now, what forms of nourishment do you usually consume?'

'Well, various fruits and vegetables or pulses - and some people eat meat and fish,' said Lewis.

Eight again searched its database for references to these foodstuffs. 'Hmmm...' it mused. 'We have no concept of any of these things in this world as far as my databank history can detect. What about minerals? Do you consume them?'

The three children again exchanged concerned glances. 'Sort of,' said Artie. 'We need small amounts of minerals like Zinc and Iron and Calcium and some vitamins in our diet - but we usually get those from inside the food.'

Eight fell silent for a few seconds - then a strange thing happened. From low-down on its body a little hatch opened, rather magically. That area, (like all parts of the machine's body), had no visible seams at all - until somehow it did. From the hatch a small scoop-like device popped out and swept up a handful of Tekktate, then promptly disappeared back inside its body resealing itself completely, (and again) quite magically. More noises began inside, this time grinding and pounding and some more sloshing.

In a low, hushed voice, as though talking to itself Eight mumbled, '...a little bit of this, extract some of that, compound this and that and this... hmmm, might be poisonous to them in those quantities... remove more of that - sprinkle some of this... well, that may just do it.'

With a loud ping, the same hatch the water came from earlier opened and on its platform were presented three small, flat discs that looked a little like biscuits.

'I believe that these, largely mineral-based discs, will safely provide you with the nutrition you need for at least part of the journey.'

Eight stood there patiently, tapping the ends of its bulky clamps together, as the children eyed up the odd snacks the machine had prepared from the dirt on the ground. Kat and Lewis looked very reluctant - but Artie, whose stomach was again rumbling, grabbed one of the biscuits and wolfed it down.

'In for a penny...' he said as he swallowed. 'Tastes not too bad, really.'

Kat and Lewis tentatively lifted the biscuits towards their mouths, eying them suspiciously. As the biscuit touched her tongue Kat grimaced.

'Tastes like metal,' she said before swallowing. After a few seconds, however, she started to look brighter and feel perkier.

'Wow!' said Artie, as he started to feel the full effects. 'Talk about an energy bar!'

Lewis looked at his friend and sister, studying them and their newfound energy before deciding it was safe to follow their lead. Once the metallic aftertaste had faded, he nodded his head in agreement as he could feel the positive effects of the strange energy-biscuit-made-from-dirt.

Artie felt as though his brain had been turbo-charged and questions flooded his mind.

'Travel by detonation?' he asked. 'What on earth does that mean?'

Eight studied the boy carefully. 'My primary function is on-demand detonation for excavation. To put it in words that you can perhaps understand - I can make bombs to create new craters and holes. As I am indestructible, sometimes I enjoy creating and detonating these bombs and let the explosions propel me where I want to go. It is an efficient and fun way to travel great distances.'

'You make bombs?' asked Lewis, somewhat fearful that their soon to be travel-companion was a walking, talking death-trap. 'How?'

'I can reconstitute Tekktate into a number of forms,' Eight replied. 'One of those forms can be made to combust under extreme pressure. Once it reaches a critical point, I expel it from my innards through one of my lower hatches before it explodes.'

Artie burst out laughing. 'So, wait a minute! You can lay bombs like a chicken lays an egg? And then if you stand close enough to it the explosion shoots you across the sky?'

'That is correct,' stated Eight, oblivious to the reason for Artie's mirth.

All three children burst out laughing uncontrollably, even Lewis. Tears ran down Artie's face as he struggled to regain control of himself.

'Now, shall we begin?' asked Eight, slightly grumpily. 'The world will not fix itself.'

Artie looked at the nothingness all around them, and at the nothingness on the horizon and thought to himself. 'On we go then. What other choice do we have?'

CHAPTER FOUR

Seas of Red

They walked mostly in silence for a while as they faced the reality of crossing such a vast distance filled with unknowns. Only the oddly isolated sound of their own footsteps and Eight's mechanical movements broke the total vacuum of sound. Lewis spent much of the initial part of the trek looking at his feet, studying how the thin veil of red Kora coursed through and washed over the ground, lapping at his boots. He noticed that it behaved the same way around Artie's feet, but with Kat it was slightly different. The red charge did not physically lap at her navy-blue trainers - it kept a small distance, as though there was an invisible buffer around his sister's feet - the red Kora even seemed to him to be afraid to get any closer, jerking away from her shoes just as it dared to get near. He presumed that, because Kat had been imbued with such a large amount of green Kora that it was protecting her somehow, and he wondered if it would last. His mind drifted as they trudged on and he wondered what the opposite of lapping was, if there even was such a thing.

'Chose Kat?' he thought to himself. 'Eight said to Kat that perhaps the machine chose her, somehow.' He would never have thought such a thing was possible - but now, here, having spoken to a walking-talking-thinking machine with its own sense of identity and personality in this weirdly frozen world, anything seemed possible.

Lewis looked at Eight's heavy mechanical feet and realised that the red Kora behaved differently with it too. Instead of lapping against, or scared of, the red charge seemed to be grabbing on tightly to Eight's feet. Each time Eight lifted one of its invisibly-piston-powered feet, strands of red became elongated and strained until they finally broke apart, fell away and re-joined the great sea of red underneath. Eight's feet seemed to very slightly tremble and shake as they fought against the red charge as it tried to cling to the machine. It was then that Lewis realised what an effort it must be for Eight - each step across the vast sea an enormous struggle and effort to simply be able to keep moving.

'This must be draining him enormously,' Lewis thought as he felt a short pang of sympathy for their new and apparently explosive companion. He wondered what they would do if the machine was not able to complete the journey and the three children were left alone to find their own way. He looked again to the horizon and still saw no sign of any structure in any direction and felt another wave of dread. Thankfully, Lewis was soon shaken from his ever-darkening inner feelings as Artie spoke.

'Eight, does the sun usually come up here, or is it always like this - not really dark but not really light either?' he asked.

'Oh yes,' replied Eight. 'Our suns work in regular cycles as I presume they do on many worlds.'

'Suns?' asked Lewis. 'Plural?'

'Ours is a trinary system; three suns,' replied the machine before continuing as though it had not been interrupted. 'At their highest it can be very bright indeed, and at their lowest it is almost completely dark. But with Time frozen it is neither. Ours are distant suns - very, very far away - if Time was to become unstuck you would see and feel that, whilst there is much light, there is very little heat.'

'Fine by me,' said Artie. 'I don't really like the heat - all that sweating and being sticky. Although…' he thought, '…water-gun fights are a lot of fun in the warm sun. And ice-cream!'

'Don't,' said Kat. 'You'll make us all hungry again. Change the subject, please.'

'What about the weather?' asked Lewis as he realised the weather is what grown-ups usually discuss when asked to change the subject. 'Does it rain here? Snow?'

'We have had many weather events in the past,' replied Eight. 'Strong winds lifted and swirled Tekktate into sand-devils and tornadoes and created moving barriers like sandstorms. As almost everything on this world cannot be damaged, they were more an inconvenient nuisance than a serious problem. They would, however, be deadly to fragile beings like you. You need not worry - it cannot happen whilst Time is frozen, and once we fix the world our weather control systems will be operational once more. Extreme, unpredictable weather is a thing of the past on Fabrakka. It no longer rains or snows or hails here unless we want it to. Which we never do.'

'Cool,' said Artie, smiling. 'Snow days on-demand!'

Eight rotated its dials and looked intently at Artie, realising that he had somewhat missed the point - the system was there to prevent disruptive weather, not allow it to be turned on and off like a tap. Eight however, said nothing out loud, despite its innate desire to scold Artie, and a new sensation grew in its inner circuits - Eight realised that it had very quickly grown accustomed to the company of these fleshy beings and was even now modifying its behaviour to spare their feelings.

'Very odd,' Eight thought to itself. 'Perhaps I am not running as I should be. I must carry out a diagnostic check of my systems soon. Perhaps the red charge draining me is also interfering with my logic circuits.' Eight suddenly felt drawn to look towards Kat and remembered the physical contact they shared and the surge of green Kora that flowed from her into it. 'Or perhaps it is something else…' it mused.

'I assume machines don't need much sleep?' asked Kat as she found herself growing tired and stifling a yawn as she continued to shuffle her feet forward.

Eight made more of its usual inner clunking and whirring sounds, which the children now knew meant it was thinking deeply. As it did so, its triangular set of dials rotated again so that the gauge was at the top.

'Sleep,' it said as the needle bounced back and forth in that familiar manner and began to quote from its in-build dictionary. 'To take the rest afforded by a suspension of bodily functions. No, we machines do not need to sleep.'

Artie, Lewis and Kat all looked at each other - all six of their eyebrows raised in alarm. The children were beginning to feel very fatigued and the possibility of the machine dragging them endlessly across the red seas without rest now felt very real.

'However…' Eight continued, '…long-term and continual operations can cause our systems to fragment. In order to maintain perfect working order we must run a defragmentation process, and this is more effectively carried out during low-power mode. I suppose that could be called sleep. My next defragmentation is scheduled to occur in 10 of your Earth years.'

The children initially sighed relief at the prospect of the machine sleeping but were then horrified when they understood they may have to wait 10 years for it to happen. Regardless, Lewis took his opportunity to ask what all three of them were thinking.

'Can we rest?' he asked. 'I'm beat.'

'Hungry,' said Kat.

'Thirsty,' said Artie.

Eight looked towards the horizon - the outline of the great city it had promised had not yet materialised despite their lengthy trudging. It looked at the children, who it thought were now rather crumpled, as they bent over and slumped onto the ground. Eight exerted another mechanised sigh.

'Fine,' it said, rather huffily. 'Here you may have a short sleep. When you awaken there will be more water and biscuits.'

Artie fell asleep before Eight had finished its sentence, and Kat drifted off shortly after - despite the discomfort of lying on the raw Tekktate. Lewis' body was physically drained but his mind was still very active and so it took him a little longer, and his sleep was quite restless. He felt as though he had slept for just a few moments when he was awoken by the sound of voices. Still very tired he lay there and listened in the hope that he might steal a few more minutes of rest.

'...so much fun...' Artie's voice said, '...and there are water-park slides, and rollercoasters and great big inflatable things to bounce across and scramble nets to climb up and huge death-slides that propel you along and French Fries and burgers and hot-dogs and sodas and ice-cream that comes in a hundred different flavours and a hundred more toppings to choose from and candy floss and then at Christmas time there are mince pies and at Easter time there are chocolate eggs filled with all sorts of different sweets or toys, and…'

Artie's enthusiastic ranting was interrupted by the familiar sound of sloshing, grinding and pinging.

'Your water and biscuits are ready,' Eight said, flatly.

Lewis slowly raised himself and properly opened his eyes. Kat and Artie were already sitting upright and were reaching for their breakfast. Or dinner. Without Time it was impossible to know which meal was which. Lewis wearily shuffled himself across the ground to join them.

'For highly fragile beings…' Eight said, '…you do seem to create and enjoy activities that put you in great peril. I would have to analyse your foodstuffs in greater detail but from your description it seems to me that you eat large quantities of very unbalanced forms of nourishment. I do wonder how your species has survived all this time.'

Kat munched her dry biscuit wishing she had not heard Artie's excited descriptions of ice-cream and chocolate. Artie, however, did not appear to mind and he had finished his biscuit and water before she had even eaten half of hers. Lewis again eyed the small disc of reconstituted dirt with distrust.

'Even prisoners get more than bread and water these days,' he said to himself with a heavy heart. Before he had finished his snack, Eight, like some sort of mechanised school teacher, commanded them.

'Let us continue,' it said. 'There is much distance still to cover.'

The three children slowly stood up and began to trudge on towards the empty horizon. The energy from the biscuits seemed to take longer to have any effect than last time, but overall, they did feel better for having rested and eaten something. It was a short time before they realised their group of four was, in fact, only three. They looked back at their makeshift camp to see that Eight had not moved very far.

'Ah,' it called out and seemed to Lewis to be acting rather sheepishly. 'It would appear that... I am unable to move. I may have underestimated the draining effect of the red Kora on my functions.'

Kat felt a great pang of sympathy for the pompous machine and rushed across to it. She laid her hands gently on its outer shell and, in a far more controlled manner than the first time, let the green charge flow from her hands into the machine. This time Eight did not go haywire, but - as it felt the power flood back into its circuits and mechanisms - it simply grabbed and gently squeezed Kat's hand with its large clamp-like appendage. The two stood for just a few seconds, girl and machine silently connected, as Eight repowered. Its three dials rotated once more so that the pressure-gauge was at the top and the needle inside rose then gently fell.

Eight made the fake clearing its non-existent throat noise again before repeating exactly the words it had said before.

'Let us continue,' it said. 'There is much distance still to cover.'

Eight strode purposefully towards the two boys and marched past them without even a glance and in a very determined manner.

'Well that's just a bit concerning,' whispered Lewis once Eight was out of earshot. 'What if Kat needs to do that every time Eight needs to make us breakfast? What if she runs out of the green stuff? This city is so, so far away - we're going to get stranded, or starve, I know it!'

Artie would, in situations like these, usually respond to Lewis with something along the lines of 'it'll be fine,' or 'you worry too much.' This time, though, Artie felt that there might be some merit to Lewis' anxiousness - and so said nothing, but simply gestured to Kat to hurry and join them. Once she had, the three children upped their pace until they had caught up with the machine, now confidently striding across the vast sea, seemingly unconcerned with the tendrils of red Kora grabbing onto its feet with every step.

As they walked on, Artie took the chance to look at the sky properly for the first time. It was, of course, the same low level of light which made it hard to see anything clearly; but if he concentrated on one area for a while, he could make out what appeared to be cloud formations. It struck him as a very odd thing that, even in low-wind days at home, the clouds would still be gently moving and shifting and changing shape into some other forms or merging together - but here, they simply hung suspended with not a single wisp altering its position or tone. It made for an odd optical illusion and that, more than anything else he had seen so far, showed Artie that Time was entirely frozen here - not just on the ground or as far as they could see but across the entire world. Artie wondered how far the Time-freeze extended. Eight mentioned their distant suns way out in their solar system - was Time frozen there too or did the light from the suns get slower and slower as it approached this world until it eventually stopped? He thought that having three suns was probably the reason why what little light they had seemed to be coming from every direction at once. It all fascinated him but made his head hurt and he was relieved when Kat, growing restless more quickly than the others, spoke and broke the silence.

'Why were you all the way out here?' she asked Eight as she looked around. 'I mean, there's nothing - absolutely nothing here.'

Eight took a short time before responding.

'On the surface of it there is nothing, that is true. But as a bomb-maker and crater-maker there is always what is underneath to consider. I was here to determine the makeup of the Tekktate in this area - to assess its density, primarily. I understand that may be a frankly, uninteresting answer to your question, but it is part of the role I fulfil on Fabrakka. For the good of all machines.'

'Oh,' said the children almost in unison, all three clearly unimpressed by Eight's dry, geological answer. They continued again in silence until, very gradually, the ground beneath their feet began to slope - then it sloped a bit more and then it dropped away and before they knew it, they were walking over undulating, rolling hills. Whilst this was harder on their legs, they were grateful there was at least some change from trudging across the same flat and featureless ground.

'Are all the machines on Fabrakka built like you?' asked Artie towards Eight rather abruptly. 'I mean, as sleek as you are on the outside, you're all sorts of mad noises on the inside. Are they all like you - bulky and analogue and... old?'

'Certainly not!' replied Eight just as bluntly. 'There are many new machines in Fabrakka capable of feats I have never seen before and whose components I must admit, I have trouble fully appreciating and understanding their composition. There is much variety amongst the many machines of Fabrakka.'

'Yeah, I'm sure...' continued Artie, '...but are they all still like you - but just more refined versions of the same underlying technology? No offence, but you mostly sound like an old steam train - and when you think it sounds like a room full of looms. We had a time like that in our world - a few centuries ago - where everything was made like that. We're way past that now though.'

Eight harrumphed mechanically before replying.

'Was this a Golden Age for your people, when you created and developed these machines? Was your world a happy, flourishing place with no conflict and where everyone wanted for nothing? Is your world now a paradise as a result of your more advanced technologies?' asked Eight.

'Well, no,' replied Artie. 'I guess it wasn't. And no, it isn't now either.'

'Perhaps, then...' said Eight, sounding again very much like a schoolteacher reprimanding an unruly pupil, '...your use of technology was mishandled over the years. Perhaps it was controlled and exploited by the wrong fleshy beings and not made to benefit all on your world. Perhaps you rushed headlong into new technologies without fully considering the risks. On Fabrakka, we have accomplished much, and all that we did accomplish benefited all machines collectively. Until v0-LT-2, this world was a wonderful, happy place of equals.'

'It certainly sounds like it was a much fairer place than our world,' said Lewis, shuddering again at the sound of v0-LT-

2's name. 'I hope we can make it that way again. I'd love to see it.'

Kat, (who was not really listening to the slightly heated conversation), yawned and groaned, feeling the effects of the biscuits wearing off. She stopped and turned, looking back towards where they had set off from. She peered at the horizon and from their more elevated position, she saw that she could see a little further than she could earlier. But the same wilderness stared back at her and she was not entirely sure how far they had come. She was just about to suggest they rested and had more to eat when Artie interrupted.

'What's that?' he said pointing at a nearby hillside. The group followed his finger and stared at the hill, and they could all see a hole in the hillside. The hole disappeared as soon as it appeared, and then reappeared again - as though it was glitching.

'Curious,' said Eight, but nothing more.

'Let's take a closer look,' said Artie and immediately started off. Kat followed closely behind, re-energised by the thought of something more interesting to investigate. Lewis and Eight followed behind them, and even they had more urgency in their steps.

The group caught up with Artie who had stopped and was staring at the hillside scratching his head.

'I'm sure it was here,' he said, sighing, looking directly at a sloped and solid mound of Tekktate. Suddenly, the hole flickered and blinked into existence once more in front of them.

'Very curious,' said Eight. 'When I first travelled out this way, I detected no such feature. However, I may have simply blasted myself past it at a great height.'

The hole continued to erratically come and go as the group surrounded it. Without warning, Artie put his head through the opening and disappeared.

'Artie!' cried Kat.

'I'm fine!' he shouted and popped his head back through the opening. 'Come take a look at this.'

Cautiously the group crouched and stepped through the gap into a small vestibule where they saw a tall, thin contraption with many lights and pipes coming out of it, and whose pipes ran around the frame of the hole. Artie gestured towards it.

'I think this machine is what's causing the hole to flicker on and off. Look, there's both red and green Kora covering its surface.'

They all looked closer at the machine, made of the same polished black restless material as Eight and the mansion machine, and could see thousands of tiny fissures of very pale red and green charge crawling all over it. Oddly, the red and green Kora never mixed - each having its own dedicated set of fissures to flow through, clearly designed to keep them apart.

'Mere conjecture you understand, and I am not one for guessing, but I believe this machine may be malfunctioning,' said Eight.

The children all looked at Eight and collectively sighed and shook their heads.

'You don't say!' said Artie, trying not to laugh.

'What do you think it is?' asked Lewis. 'Is it some sort of security system, designed to camouflage the hole?'

'That does, on the face of it, appear to be its purpose,' said Eight as it clunked around the tall machine, studying it more closely and knocking on its outer shell. 'I have, however, never seen a machine with quite this style of construction. It is extremely rudimentary, and... I am not entirely sure that it has any form of brain or cognitive functions.'

'Why would something want to hide this place?' asked Lewis.

'There's only one way to find out,' said Artie as he began walking down the tunnel adjoining the vestibule.

'I urge caution,' called Eight loudly after him. 'There is much about this situation that gives a sense of unease.'

Artie heard, but did not listen and carried on down the tunnel, which as it turned out was rather short. It was not long before his outburst travelled back up the tunnel towards Eight and Lewis who quickened their pace when they heard it.

'Wow!' Artie yelled as he stepped into a very large cavern that was surprisingly bright for being in the ground. Great lights hung from the roof of the cavern, flickering erratically on and off just as the camouflaged opening had been. Dotted all around the cavern was an assortment of bizarre-looking contraptions, and in front of him were strips of grass and dirt patches - very much like the allotments on the outskirts of his own small village at home. Multiple pens fenced off with wooden planks and wooden gates were arranged off to one side.

'It's a farm!' cried Kat. 'Or at least… it used to be.'

Eight stood and looked at the farm, experiencing an entirely new sensation - the machine was completely dumbfounded and struggled, for a few moments, to find the words.

'I… I… these materials are most odd,' it said as it took a closer look at one of the fence-posts. 'What is this?'

'It's wood,' said Lewis very matter-of-fact. 'On our world we have life forms called trees that grow big and tall and then we cut them down to use their wood to build things. It's what they are naturally made of.'

'You cut them down?' asked Eight, horrified.

'Oh, it's not like that,' said Kat. 'Trees aren't like you and I - they can't think or feel anything.'

'Ah,' said Eight, not entirely sure it did fully understand. 'They are dumb and have no other purpose.'

'Well, actually,' continued Lewis. 'They absorb poisonous gases from our air and give back the oxygen we need to breathe. So… they have an essential purpose.'

Eight's innards whirred again and made a new set of unpleasant noises the children had not yet heard.

'And yet you still cut them down?' asked Eight. 'You three children seem like pleasant beings, mostly, but the actions of your species make my logic circuits seize.'

'The machine has a point,' said Artie as he strode away to investigate one of the bizarre-looking contraptions. 'There's a symbol on this one' he called back. 'I think it's wheat... and this one has some sort of berry on it.'

'There's a symbol scratched into this fence-post too,' called Lewis. 'It looks a bit like a pig. I don't think whoever drew this was a very good artist though.'

'I do not know these symbols,' said Eight peering at the crude drawing. 'This was not made by any machine of Fabrakka. As you children recognise these etchings, I can only conclude that this is the work of another one of you humans.'

'The professor!' exclaimed all three children at once.

'Who is this professor?' asked Eight, whirring.

'Well...' began Kat, '...we're not really sure. But it was in his house that we found the machine that brought us here. He's been missing for a very long time. I think we may have found where he has been all these years.'

'Is there anything worse...' began Lewis as his stomach rumbled, '...than being on a farm designed to make food for a human to eat, when there's nothing left to be eaten.'

The children looked around the cavern. Every pen was empty, every strip of dirt barren and every machine silent.

'Machines made by a human to make things that machines do not need,' pondered Eight. 'Well, perhaps Kat would like to try to restart one of the machines and by doing so we may learn more? Carefully...'

Kat nodded and strode across to the nearest machine, which even more so than the machine in the mansion, was a twisted mass of pipes, pumps, bulbs and gauges. It had the symbol of an apple crudely scratched into its surface - clearly not all of these machines were made entirely from indestructible Tekktate. Kat laid her hands on the machine's surface and let some of the green Kora flow from her into it. The machine shuddered and jolted and began banging as though it was going to explode. Kat stepped cautiously backwards as the banging gradually subsided and the machine began to rev and churn. Suddenly a great sound rang out.

'COCKADOODLEDOO!' it bellowed with a breathy quality like the whistle from a steam train. Kat watched as green power flowed from one machine to the next and then the next. The devices were all now clearly connected, and the cacophony of banging, grinding and churning made the children cover their ears. To their amazement the conveyor belts attached to each machine began moving and within just a few seconds apples, various berries, wheat, corn and assortments of nuts all appeared in surprisingly generous quantities.

'Food!' cried Artie as he instinctively grabbed an apple and bit into it.

'Wait!' urged Lewis. 'Shouldn't we test it first? What if it's all rotten and no good?'

'I am testing it,' said Artie through mouthfuls of apple. 'And it's delicious.'

Suddenly, from another tunnel at the back of the cavern a line of small machines waddled out carrying containers that were almost as big as they were. They each positioned themselves at the end of one of the conveyors and placed the containers to catch all the food as it dropped off the end of the belts.

Artie laughed, recalling an old advert from television that he had seen on a compilation clip-show featuring very similar looking machines. He thought the advert may have been for mashed potatoes or something, but the machines of this farm moved more robotically and were nowhere near as funny. As soon as the containers were filled, the waddling machines trooped off and returned with empty containers. They took no notice of Kat or Lewis or even of Artie as he waved his hands in front of them to provoke some form of recognition or reaction.

'Very curious,' said Eight as it watched the funny little contraptions go about their business. 'I do not believe that these machines have any form of higher processing either - I believe they may have been programmed with physical functionality only. I have never seen such a thing on Fabrakka. Is this common on your world?'

Kat looked at Eight wryly. 'Not really,' she said.

'Over here!' shouted Artie. Kat looked around to see that Lewis and Artie had slunk away whilst Eight was talking and had further explored the extents of the farm. Artie emerged through another opening at the far side of the farm and he seemed to be clutching something. Kat rushed over to join them whilst Eight clunked after her.

'There's a study and a small bedroom just beyond here. Filled with books and papers and instruments. Look!' said Artie as he presented the group a rather tatty book.

Kat opened the cover and saw in very neat handwriting the words 'My Time in the World of Machines by J. B. Alexander.'

'No doubt about it,' started Lewis. 'The professor was here. I guess we weren't the first humans on Fabrakka after all.'

Eight made a new sound that to Lewis and Artie meant very little. Kat however, knew exactly what Eight was feeling. The indestructible machine was afraid.

CHAPTER FIVE

A Jolt in Time

Artie turned out the tiny cupboard and grabbed the two small, shabby knapsacks therein. Within just a few minutes both bags were stuffed full of food and he was standing ready to leave.

Lewis looked at Artie, standing impatiently, tapping his foot and seemingly desperate to continue their onward journey to the city.

'Hold on a minute,' said Lewis, more towards Kat than the others. 'We haven't fully explored this place. Let's think about this for a second... clearly the professor spent a lot of time here - and judging by the tatty state of everything in here, he likely stayed put for a long time. What if there's more stuff here we can use? What if there's more information? What if there's some sort of machine that can send us home?'

Kat perked up at the mention of home and her eyes sparkled. She felt that if she knew they could return home safely, she would rather enjoy this whole adventure - but the thought of not being able to have her old life again made her feel uneasy and hollow inside.

'Yes,' she said. 'We really should make sure we've covered every inch of the farm.'

Artie sighed a little but knew they were talking sense and so did not voice any objections. He had a burning desire to see Eight's great city and, in truth, was not yet ready to go home. He had always dreamed of having great adventures with his best friends and now that he was living such an adventure, he wanted to make sure he savoured every moment. Plus, he knew what he must find and maybe, just maybe, it really did exist in this other world.

Eight whirred and clunked once more. 'There is much logic to your proposal Lewis. I have also determined that perhaps I should attempt to communicate with this facility - there may indeed be answers within it that can help us understand more about this professor and his ability to travel between our two worlds.'

Lewis scoffed a handful of nuts as the group of four nodded collectively in agreement and the mashed potato machines (as Artie had taken to calling them) continued busying around them.

'If you're going to talk to the farm…' Artie began, '…try to turn it off. We have loads of food now and the noise is driving me crazy.'

Eight made another new noise. Artie thought that if he did not know any better, he would have thought the machine had almost laughed, although it was a nervous one. Eight scanned the farm, looking for something that may be a communication interface. Had this been a facility designed and built by a machine, it would have known exactly what sort of thing to look for - but as this was designed and built by a human, the machine was understandably confused. Kat, who was now standing near a wall on the far left-hand side of the farm, beckoned to Eight to join her. She was standing next to a single metal rectangular plate fastened to the wall - small slats were visible near the top of the plate and a single button positioned near the bottom. She pushed the button and talked into the slats.

'Hello?' she asked, feeling a little bit silly. 'Is that the farm?'

They waited. There was no response. Kat pushed the button again but before she could speak the slats started to crackle in response.

'Professor?' came the crackly reply.

The feminine voice took her aback slightly. She moved her hand away from the button and turned to Eight.

'What should we say?' she whispered. 'Should we pretend to be the professor? Maybe it won't talk to us unless we're him?'

Eight hummed, thinking. 'I understand your logic, Kat - and I have no direct experience of this type of thing - but in my opinion, deceitfulness seems a risky strategy.'

Kat nodded in understanding but then pushed the button and said in her best grown-up manly voice, 'Yes.'

'Where have you been?' the panel crackled. 'My internal chronometer stopped and seems all mixed up. How long were you away?'

Eight rotated its head back and forth disapprovingly as Kat continued.

'I was delayed,' lied Kat. 'I'm sorry. What happened while I was gone?'

The panel crackled again but no words came out for a time. Eight surmised that the farm was a bit of a slow thinker and maybe not very well constructed.

'I am not sure,' replied the farm. 'You were here and then you were not here. I thought you would come back but then you did not come back. I went to sleep and then I could not wake up. Until now. Why did you leave so suddenly?'

'It was... unavoidable,' lied Kat again. 'Tell me, what other machines are here now?'

'That is a strange question professor,' crackled the farm. 'Everything is much the same as you left it. There is just me and the helpers and the security system. Except we are no longer in peak condition - I do not believe the security system is running optimally.'

'Tell me what happened,' said Kat.

There was another prolonged pause before the farm replied.

'When you left me, everything continued as normal for a long time. I maintained the machinery and security, and we produced and collected the food at the same rate as normal for your consumption. Without you here, the food supplies grew very plentiful but began to rot. I am afraid the animals died without your attention. I decided to shut down the machinery and the helpers until you returned. For a very long time there was just security and I - and I was alone because you did not give security a brain and I had nothing else to do and there were no other machines to talk to. One day, the silver energy that powered me changed and became red and hurtful and made me feel very sleepy. That is all I know. Are you back for good, professor? Will everything return to normal? Will you bring more animals to the farm? I miss the funny noises they made. I missed you professor. No machine should be without its Maker, professor.'

Kat felt a great wave of sympathy for the lonely machine - and felt even worse that she had lied to it - but they had, through her deceit, obtained the information they needed. There was no other machine here that could send them home. Kat gently pushed the button once more.

'I hope to fully return soon,' she lied gruffly. 'Then everything can return to normal.' Kat paused before continuing as she suddenly had an idea. 'But now I must leave again for a short time. While I am away, I am setting you a great task that I know you can complete. You must design the best brains you can for security and for the helpers. Security must be able to diagnose and fix any problems with its systems by itself. Each helper must have a completely different brain from all the others so that we can tell them apart. I will review all your designs when I return and then together, we will evolve these machines into far better machines. Do you understand?'

'Oh yes,' replied the farm. 'That is a wonderful task. I will begin at once and await your return.'

'Perhaps, while I am away...' continued Kat, '...you should halt the machines and all the helpers - to make sure you have enough power to work on your designs.'

The clanking and pounding of the farm machinery ceased almost instantly and each helper froze mid-stride.

'Have a wonderful journey, professor,' crackled the farm with renewed glee. 'I am glad you are safe, for I was worried you had come to harm.'

Kat rubbed her throat which had become sore from her pretend, deep, grown-up man-voice.

'Don't,' she said to Eight, knowing that it was about to reprimand her for all her fibs.

'I understand the meaning of the word - but lying is something I have never encountered on Fabrakka... and it seems you are an accomplished liar...' Eight said, '...but I do believe that you have now left that machine with a worthy purpose and... hmmm, I cannot quite find the correct word.'

'Hope,' said Kat.

Eight again moved its head - this time up and down rather than side to side - its servo mechanisms hidden by its sleek exterior gently whirring as it did so.

'There is much about human behaviour I have yet to fully appreciate,' said Eight as they walked across the now calm farm to re-join the boys.

'Well, we've looked everywhere,' said Lewis glumly whilst stuffing the professor's tatty notebook into his knapsack. 'There's nothing else here - certainly no other machinery. I guess we should get moving.'

The group again agreed with collective nodding of heads and made their way back through the short tunnel and past the security system. As they exited through the glitching hole in the hillside, Kat wondered what sort of personality security may have in the future - and if she would ever see this place again. She looked across the rolling hills towards the empty horizon, still unable to see the great city, but consoled herself by taking an apple from Artie's knapsack and munching it as they again began their trek.

It was a couple of hours before anyone said anything - their time at the farm seemed to have drained them of their verve - the excitement of something new and a glimpse into the professor's life had given way to the disappointment of no homeward-bound machine or further information that could help them understand Fabrakka's predicament. Kat began to feel a growing sense of remorse for her untruths - what if her plan to give the lonely farm some hope backfired and she had simply given it an impossible and incompletable task that frustrated it and made it feel worse? She tried to shake the feeling of dread that crept over her, and thankfully the changes to the ground underfoot made her forget all about the farm. The ground had changed from rolling hills to steep inclines, where natural steps had formed, and the group had to alter their stepping style to make progress. For the children this was easy enough, although a little tiring, but for Eight whose legs were fighting against the red tendrils of Kora it proved more of a challenge.

Lewis knew that it could not be true, but he could not shake the feeling that the great city felt even further away than when they first began their trek. He thought perhaps that it was just an illusion, more of a twisted feeling than an optical one, a consequence of there being no measurable Time.

'Perhaps... a short... break,' Eight said with fractured whirrs. 'You children must be growing tired... and in need of further... sustenance.'

'I'm ok,' said Lewis as he looked down the steep hillside which now more resembled a gorge. He noticed that, a little further along the hillside, the red energy seemed to be concentrating in denser streams at the bottom of the gorge. In the areas where it seemed most dense it pulsed and sparked far more brightly.

'I'm fine too,' said Artie as he unwrapped an orange. 'I could keep going for a while if need be.'

'Me too,' said Kat, who looked at Eight and noticed that it did not look at all okay. She saw that, as it stood still, the red tendrils' hold on Eight's feet were less fleeting and more persistent.

'I... insist,' said Eight as it ungainly plonked itself down on the ground, great plumes of steam hissing out of every invisible seam as it did so. 'We must ensure you have... the correct levels of energy... and nourishment.'

Eight sighed mechanically and its innards made a strange combination of very awkward sounding noises. Kat thought that the machine did not seem to be functioning terribly well.

'I do miss travelling by detonation,' it said. 'This... walking... everywhere - is most inefficient.'

Lewis and Artie exchanged a look, and without needing any words they continued the conversation they had had after breakfast when Kat had to restart the drained machine.

'Ok,' said Lewis as he began to rummage around in the knapsack for some food. 'I suppose we could stop for...'

Lewis collapsed to the ground as a great rumble erupted overhead and the ground shook so violently underneath it knocked him off his feet. A rush of air flew violently into the faces of all three children and they took deep breaths as the staleness of Fabrakka was blown away and replaced with the freshness of a cool spring day. The half-light bloomed into full daylight in an instant, and in just a few seconds the world was transformed from stale, dark and hushed to fresh, light and thunderous. As soon as it had begun, it stopped - the air became stale again as though sucked away by an enormous vacuum, the light froze, and the noise and vibrations halted sharply.

'What... Was... That?' yelled Lewis, panicking and struggling back to his feet.

Kat freed herself from Artie's tight grasp - he had instinctively grabbed her and pulled her close as the ferocious shaking threatened to knock them both to the ground as it had done Lewis.

Eight began to stand, then realised that it could not quite manage to do so, and so slumped again onto the red-infused Tekktate.

'I believe...' began Eight, '...that *that* was Time.'

'Time for what?' asked Lewis, unsure of the machine's meaning.

'Just Time,' continued Artie, quickly grasping Eight's point. 'For a short period of time - there was actual Time. Stuff happening. Moving. Not stuck.'

'It's light,' said Kat, staring at the sky which was now much brighter and a rather pleasant shade of bluish-purple. 'The clouds are all in different positions now too.'

'Yes,' said Eight. 'It is indeed much, much lighter, which suggests to me that we experienced a lot of Time in those few seconds. A heavily concentrated burst, if you will. Perhaps hours packed into seconds.'

'Cool,' said Artie. 'The light will make the rest of the journey a bit easier. I see what you mean about the temperature though Eight,' he continued as he shivered and rubbed his arms. 'Did it actually get lighter but noticeably colder for a few seconds?'

'The ambient temperature did indeed briefly drop significantly...' said the machine, thinking deeply and clunking as heavily and as noisily as the children had ever heard it, '...but I believe that is the least of our worries. Fabrakka may be stuck, but it is clearly more unstable than I had anticipated. These jolts in Time may become more and more unpredictable and possibly more violent. Or, instead, we may experience a long period before another jolt occurs - if one ever does. There is no way to currently predict their events - not without more data.'

'Wonderful,' said Lewis sarcastically, to mask that he was in fact, rather afraid.

Eight held out an outstretched, still steaming and gently hissing arm towards Kat, who grabbed it and helped the machine back to its unsteady feet with another nod of acknowledgement.

The machine and the girl stood and looked at the horizon again, towards where the city should be, the nothingness now far more visible in the lightness of the frozen day.

'How is your energy?' asked Kat.

'Oh, fine, fine...' replied the machine unconvincingly. 'There is no need, just yet, for you to work your green magic on my innards. Soon perhaps.'

Kat said nothing but wondered why the machine seemed reluctant to let her infuse it with another dose of green Kora. Do machines feel pride, she wondered - or was it simply that Eight was concerned she would not have enough green power for an emergency, should one occur?

'Can we get moving?' asked Lewis who had also started to rub his arms as the residual cold from the short blast meant he struggled to get warm again. 'I think we need...'

The group were all thrown to the floor as another great rumble erupted overhead and the ground shook violently beneath, and more cool air blasted into their faces. Alongside her feet - now sprawled out in front of her - Kat saw a large crack appear instantly which then grew and grew at such a rapid pace that she could not shift her legs away in time. Before she knew it, the crack was a gaping wide chasm and she fell - down, down, down into the darkness, scrambling as she fell to grab onto anything she could.

The rumbling and shaking grew more and more intense and frequent - and the ground, as quickly as it had torn itself apart - knitted itself back together with an ear-splitting crash. Again, there was complete silence and stillness.

'Kat!' yelled Lewis, raking his hands through the Tekktate after his sister who was now nowhere to be seen. Lewis scrambled back to his feet and turned pleadingly to Artie whose mouth was hanging wide open in shock.

'Whatdowedo-whatdowedo-whatdowedo?' panicked Lewis.

Artie stood and stared at the ground where just a moment ago Kat lay. The red Kora was throbbing even more erratically than usual. Artie tried to find the words - but nothing came out.

'This is most unfortunate,' said Eight, also staring at the patch of ground now missing a Kat.

'UNFORTUNATE?' yelled Lewis at the machine. 'She's gone!' Tears formed in his eyes, mostly because of the raw anger raging through him.

'Let's not… let's not jump to any conclusions,' said Artie who was now starting to regain his usual sense of calm. 'Eight, what are the chances she has survived?'

Eight whirred, this time largely silently - a sign that it was carrying out very complex calculations.

'Impossible to know accurately,' Eight replied eventually. 'Little is known about this area. However, Kat seems a resourceful girl - if she has survived, she will surely make her best efforts to find her way back to us. I believe our best course of action is to wait here.'

'WAIT here?' asked Lewis, growing even angrier. 'Do NOTHING?'

Eight did not reply. It began to rotate its head towards Lewis but suddenly stopped after just a few degrees of motion.

Artie stepped closer towards the machine and prodded it.

There was no reaction.

He looked at the red tendrils of Kora crawling over Eight's feet unopposed and realised that the negative charge was now covering more than just its feet - it had made its way up the machine's heavy legs and was starting to search its blackened body for a way into Eight's innards.

Great plumes of steam shot out of every seamless opening of the machine, narrowly missing Artie.

The machine was completely drained, and the two boys were now all alone.

CHAPTER SIX

Kat in the Caverns

Kat looked up at the solid Tekktate covering the hole from which she had slipped through. She was relieved she had not fallen all that far, and the hole had turned into a slope that gradually levelled itself out as she slid. As a result she had not really hurt herself, but her hands smarted a little where she had tried in vain to grab some sort of hold as she slid. The blunted Tekktate had broken the skin of her palms, but nowhere nearly as badly as would have happened from a similar fall in normal dirt at home.

'Lewis!' she yelled up towards the darkened roof that she could barely see. 'Artie?' She waited but there was no response. Her eyes had not yet had time to adjust and she realised how unfair it was to have been given the gift of total daylight just moments ago and have it taken away and replaced by even darker darkness. Kat had never been afraid of the dark - her mother had told her that there were no such things as ghosts or ghouls or monsters under her bed and she had always believed whatever her mother had told her. But this was a new world that her mother did not know - what sort of creatures might be here? They already knew of one evil in this world that had caused great harm, and maybe it was not alone.

She shivered a little at the childish thoughts growing in her mind as she looked around the blackness.

'Pull yourself together, girl,' she said inwardly, and sternly. 'You're fine.'

'Eight!' she yelled out, now with greater urgency as she failed to convince herself. Again, she waited, and again there was no reply. She wondered if another of Tekktate's unique properties was that it dampened sounds completely.

She looked around the darkness once more hoping that her eyes would adjust - and that she would be able to make out some little details - but they did not adjust at all - complete darkness is all she continued to see.

'There is nothing to be afraid of,' she again told herself, and this time she did feel a growing inner calmness as her logical brain caught up. 'See? You are fine. Now... what to do?'

She wondered what the correct course of action was - stay put in the hope of being rescued or try to find her own way out? She knew that, without Time, Eight would be unable to disrupt the Tekktate and she was convinced that the machine was now running low on power.

'The silly arrogant contraption!' she exclaimed. 'Why did it not let me boost it? Maybe then it would have enough power to get me out of this hole.'

She felt she had every right to be angry with the machine, but she also knew that even a fully powered Eight was no guarantee of rescue. Even its biggest, most powerful bomb may not be enough to break through Time and disrupt the ground.

'Time...' she thought. 'Did Time restart? Is it still happening?' The ground had swallowed her up so quickly that she had no idea if Time had returned to normal above ground or if it was just another jolt and had again stopped dead. She looked around the darkness and realised that if Time was now behaving normally, she would have no way to tell. Or did she? She bent down and grabbed a handful of Tekktate and let it fall between the fingers of one hand with her other hand waiting beneath. She presumed that the Tekktate hung in the air or fell so slowly as her lower hand felt nothing for what seemed like an age. Eventually a few lonely shards started to spatter across her palms.

'Well, that confirms that,' she said to herself. 'No use waiting around for rescue. I'm sure I'll find a way out of here, somehow.'

She flung both arms out in front of her, and wishing herself good luck, took a half step forward. Immediately her hands touched a solid wall and she stopped abruptly.

'Not that way, then,' she mused. She turned 180 degrees and laid her back against the wall and stared into the blackness ahead. Gingerly, she stepped forward another half-step and her right foot found the ground. She stepped forward with her left - it found nothing but air - and she almost fell, wobbling at the edge of what she presumed was a thin ledge.

'I must have landed on a precipice,' she said to herself through heavy breathing. She was not sure if it was lucky that she managed to stop on something so thin after her fall, or unlucky that she now had to make her way along such a dangerous path. She rotated herself 90 degrees and stood for a moment, again staring into the darkness.

'No,' she thought. 'That's not the way to do this.' She rotated herself another 90 degrees and gently raised her hands out in front of her until they met the wall of Tekktate. She laid her palms on the surface and realised that it felt much smoother and glassier than the Tekktate beneath her feet or any above ground she had felt so far. With her hands firmly laid on the wall, she slowly crabbed left along the thin precipice using the wall as her guide.

She did this for what felt like hours - but really it was only a handful of minutes. She realised that without even a dull light, or the group's voices, frozen Time in the dark was impossible to gauge. After a short while longer she did feel as though her eyes must be adjusting - small but shiny glints of red light became more and more obvious coursing across the Tekktate showing that it was in fact much glassier, and with more defined striations that seemed to tumble their way down the rockface. The red grew brighter and brighter as she edged her way along and soon her eyes began to smart with the bright pulsing of the red Kora.

'Why... I do believe the red power is much more exposed in the Tekktate down here.' She stopped and ran her fingers gently across and down the wall, following one of the striations as it plunged downwards. 'Has this been cut?' she wondered as she followed the angle of a protrusion, which she swore was at a perfect continuous 30 degrees.

Suddenly she remembered the broken skin on her palms as a sharp bolt of red charge shot out from the wall into one of the cuts.

'Ow!' she yelled as she looked down at her hands, ready to scold the red charge for its unnecessary and unruly behaviour - but before she could say anything further, a green tendril of Kora shot back from her palm and slammed the red charge back into the wall from whence it came. She grimaced as the green power broke through her skin - it did not hurt her the same way the red charge did but emerging from beneath her broken skin like that was not a terribly pleasant feeling.

She looked along the ridge into the darkness, which was now glowing slightly - the red charge illuminating at least a few metres ahead of her. She sighed and carried on, with her hands now more gingerly in contact with the wall of Tekktate, as the red and green powers continued their painful war in the small gap of stale air between her palms and the rockface.

Her left foot suddenly found nothing, and she banged her head as the roof of the cavern dropped unexpectedly lower. She steadied herself and crouched, squinting in the red dullness to see what changes lay ahead of her. The ledge was turning slightly, and the tunnel ahead was more cramped than the space she had been moving in until now. She gently dropped onto all fours and started to crawl her way into the tunnel - her bright blue jeans giving little protection for her knees. The raw Tekktate on the ground did not have the smooth, glassy feel of the wall and the war between the exposed green charge in her hands and the red raged even more violently with every shuffle forward. Tears began to form in her eyes with the smarting pain and she wiped them away with the back of her hand and again gave herself a good talking to before grave doubts began to creep into her mind.

'How do I even know if I've moved off in the right direction?' she thought to herself. 'What if this is the wrong way and I end up even further away from the city than we were?' Fears tumbled into her brain and she slowed. Finally, she convinced herself that any direction that led to above ground was the right direction and if she had to repeat part of her journey so be it. Maybe she would end up back at the farm? Maybe she would have a chance to apologise to the farm for giving it such an impossible task and for lying to it?

She felt solidness pinch her on both sides of her hips and she realised that the tunnel was becoming even thinner. She squeezed through as quickly as she could, panicking slightly at the thought of becoming stuck, and hoping amongst hope that the tunnel did not become even tighter. She was relieved to see that the tunnel widened significantly after the pinch point, but crestfallen that it then split into multiple forks. All the options open to her initially looked identical - the same narrow openings - although as she looked more intently it appeared as though one tunnel might allow her to be able to stand up a little more. She was just about to choose that route when a glint of something caught her eye down one of the other tunnels. She stared into it, hoping to catch the glint of whatever it was, but for a time there was nothing. As her eyes again adjusted, she realised that it was a gentle and very dull glow - deep green in colour - and illuminated the dog-leg in the tunnel that stopped her from seeing anything more.

'Green...' she thought excitedly and started to crawl towards it with renewed pace. She quickly squeezed herself around the dog-leg and instinctively shut her eyes to protect them from the brightness of the green light that flooded the end of the tunnel. She did not even notice the war raging beneath her palms as the green charge in her body and the red coursing through the ground fought and blistered her skin.

The tunnel ended in a bowl and in its centre a pool of the brightest and densest emerald green Kora Kat had ever seen. In such concentrations it had a completely different luminance that made it hard for her to open her eyes fully.

She squinted to look at the pool, but it was too bright to look directly at, so instead she studied the edges which were moving in what seemed to be a rhythmic pattern. All around the pool tendrils of green charge arced, like water jets being shot from one of those fancy fountains in shopping centres where they dance to music and leap over one another. She had seen one once, when she was quite young, on a trip to London - her small village did not even have a shopping centre, never mind one with an elaborate water fountain. As hypnotic as the arcing and playful green Kora was, it was not the thing that grabbed her attention the most. Around the edge of the pool there was a continuous gap, like an empty moat around a castle, and on the other side a concentration of red Kora that butted up against the gap. The red power raged ferociously in waves against the gap, as though it was trying to break through. Every now and again a single tendril of red Kora would try its luck and leap across the gap, only for a branch of green to break free from its choreographed pattern and slam the red backwards, purifying the gap - both edges of which sparked even more furiously with every failed attack and successful defence. The energy coming from both power sources was so fierce that Kat surmised that Time must have no power over them - perhaps it was even the other way around, perhaps these forms of power could somehow influence Time?

What she did next, she did so without thinking, and as though it was the most natural thing in the world. She plunged her smarting hands as deep into the centre of the green pool as she could and let the green energy flow into her. Instantly her hands tingled and felt wonderful, the smarting pain was gone, and she felt an instant calm wash over her. Her throbbing, anxious brain eased, and she sat there, bent on her knees with her hands soaking in green Kora having never felt more relaxed and never more connected to this wondrous world that, at all costs, she must fix and restore to its previous perfect glory. As her soul became completely at peace, she realised that in the back of her mind something new was forming. Initially she ignored it, thinking she would address it later after this wonderful feeling had eased - but the feeling of total tranquillity did not ease - it kept flowing wave after wave after wave. Whatever was forming in her mind also kept growing and she switched her focus, for just a second, to see what it was.

It was a map. A map not drawn with surface lines and symbols and contours but with something far deeper, as though she had been somehow responsible, aeons ago, for birthing this world. She now knew exactly where she was, and she knew exactly where to go to escape the tunnels.

Reluctantly, she withdrew her hands from the soothing mass of green Kora and retreated along the tunnel to the forks. With no hesitation, she chose a path and set off down the new tunnel with renewed vigour. Her mind was at ease and she was calm - with no concern that, soon, she would find the exit firmly drawn in her mind.

After some time, her hands felt a slight change in the rockface and ground, and that took her by surprise because it did not exactly correlate to the map in her head. She felt a little uneasy that what her mind knew, and what her body felt - were not quite the same. She pressed on regardless, but now paying more attention to the physical sensations her fingers felt as they traced the outlines of the caves and tunnels. The Tekktate had changed - it was no longer in its raw, cut form - instead it formed very distinguishable shapes - those of pipes, tubes and cylinders - and these were arranged in a regular, deliberate pattern.

'Something made this…' she thought as her hands traced what was clearly a pipeline and one that was leading somewhere in particular. She dismissed the map in her head, temporarily, and followed the pipeline which was gradually becoming smoother, glassier and better formed as though something had taken great care when sculpting it. The pipes became intertwined with wiry things, and those became intertwined with caps, levers and funnels. The whole tunnel was, inch by inch, becoming an enormous machine - a machine whose purpose Kat could not fathom. She progressed more slowly, taking in the tunnel that was no longer just a tunnel - it was now more like the inside cylinder of some vast mechanism. She spied something in the distance that was unmistakable - a row of bulbs and she realised that if she let loose just a little green Kora, perhaps she could light her way.

'I've had quite enough of this darkness, thank you very much,' she said to herself as she laid her hands on a clutch of tubes containing wiry strands that she hoped led directly to one of those bulbs. It did, and although the bulb did not give off much light, it was enough for her to see the spider-web of tunnels that now lay before her. She was not concerned by the possibilities - her map trumped all of those, but she also knew instinctively that they all led to and converged at the same location. She carried on, choosing any tunnel, until it opened into the vast cavern that she knew was there.

She gasped as she saw the sight in front of her. She knew, via the green Kora, of the great space that *was* the cavern but nothing of what was *in* the cavern itself - an enormous construction in progress - or at least, was in progress until Time had frozen. Great pillars rose out of the ground, foundations of structures not yet built ran around the perimeter and criss-crossed the cavern floor and huge glassy walls in polished blackened Tekktate loomed down from a great height. Kat stood and stared at the underground city from her elevated position above, not quite believing what her eyes were telling her.

It was a few minutes of staring before she realised that she was right to question her eyes - they were not giving her the whole truth. She looked intently at the edges of the structures and saw that they were roughened in the way Tekktate usually was not, as though they had broken off. The foundations were uneven - not regular and precise in the manner you would expect from machine constructions. It all felt just a little bit wrong to Kat and at odds with what she thought this world was - until it suddenly dawned on her.

'It's not a new city being built at all,' she exclaimed. 'It's an ancient one being excavated!' She knew instinctively that she was correct, but further questions flooded her mind. She thought back to all the conversations with Eight trying to pick apart the details in search for answers.

'But why would a race of machines, with ancestral memory - that knows everything that had ever happened on this world - cover up a great city? And then dig it up again? It doesn't make sense...' she thought. 'What am I missing?'

A wave of horror washed over her as she considered the possibility that Eight had lied to her. She struggled with that thought and could not make it sit comfortably within her.

'No,' she said to herself. 'That's not it - I don't believe that silly machine is capable of lying - or even of misleading me. But does that mean the machines don't even know this place exists?'

The possibilities swirled around her brain and the great calmness she had felt sitting by the pool felt like a lifetime ago.

Kat could not shake the feeling that she was locked out of a deep secret of this ancient world - one known only to some, not all, machines. Eight had told her that, until v0-LT-2, this world was one of total unity, openness and harmony - but the machine was very wrong. This world was split by dark, ancient secrets.

CHAPTER SEVEN

The Upturned Tree

Kat scrambled, as carefully as she could, down into the cavern and made her way across the floor to the nearest exposed foundations of the ancient city. The scale of it took her a little while to accept - she felt so tiny as she stood in the midst of the walls that now loomed up all around her. She ran her fingers gently across the corners where two walls met - the Tekktate bizarrely rough and crumbled - but not actually *crumbling* no matter how hard she pressed her hands against it. The dim lights of the bulbs she had ignited with her green charge were just enough to create shadows, and it was only then as she entered one of the largest dark pools the light created, that she realised there was a great object hanging menacingly in the stale air above her.

She looked up cautiously to see a huge lump of Tekktate - jet-black but erratically throbbing with a thin film of red Kora - suspended in mid-air. Kat, rather ungainly, hauled herself up onto a section of wall and looked up and across the desolate cavern to see that there were several lumps of various sizes, all hanging suspended in a cluster. She walked along the top of the section of wall - which was precariously thin in places - and she needed on occasion to use her arms to keep her balance. A wave of alarm suddenly hit her as she realised that another jolt in Time could cause the lumps to drop without warning and crush her before she could do anything. Flustered by the thought, she lost her footing and crashed to the ground, backwards, cursing herself for her lack of concentration.

'You daft thing!' she yelled, scolding herself. 'You can't just wobble every time you get curious about something that's off in this mad, frozen world.' She sat upright and dusted herself down before continuing. 'Besides, you don't even know if these great lumps were actually falling down or being shot up into the air when Time froze...'

She leapt back to her feet, and - quickly checking that she was, in fact, unhurt (and of course not actually dusty) - looked around at the walls that now hemmed her in the enclosed area into which she had just fallen. She was preparing to try to clamber up another section of wall to escape when something glistened in the corner of her eye. She turned and peered at this new structure - a shining black, twisted sight that her eyes and brain could not figure out.

It was a tree - sticking out of the ground perfectly straight upwards - but with a trunk that was so tightly twisted at the base it looked like it was strangling itself - and so wildly everywhere at the top it seemed to go in every direction a hundred times over. At least, a tree is the closest thing her brain could make it out to be, but as she crept closer to the distorted mass, she realised it was not a tree at all.

'Of course it isn't a tree... are there even such things on Fabrakka?' she wondered as she remembered that Eight had no idea what wood was at the farm. 'Anyway, if it had been a tree it would be an upside-down one. All these thin and twisted bits going in every direction look more like tangled roots than branches. Although I suppose some trees might look almost the same no matter which way up they were.'

She looked through the gaps in the twisted roots or branches and saw two large lumps of polished Tekktate hanging from them, just as overly large apples might do from a real tree. She had to fight her way around the spindles of rootbranch, (as she had decided to call it), to get close enough to examine the lumps - the rootbranch poked and pulled at her dark red-flecked hair as she weaved in and out of the dense mass. Finally she was close enough to one of the lumps and reached up, stretching as fully onto her tiptoes as she could and grabbed it - pulling it down closer to her. The lump came towards her surprisingly easily and she saw that the rootbranch connected to it was elongating like an elastic band does when pulled.

'This looks familiar...' she mused as her brain tried to work it all out. She turned the lump in another direction and spun it all around and then it suddenly hit her.

'It's a foot!' she cried. 'It looks almost exactly like one of Eight's feet! But bigger...' She flipped the foot over and saw that there were three symbols stamped on the 'soles' - symbols she could not read. From deep inside her somewhere, she felt the same sensation she had at the pool of green Kora, where she had been completely connected to the world and where the map had formed in her head like a long-lost friend saying hello again. It frustrated her that she could not decipher these symbols because she felt that she should be able to - just as naturally as she was able to breathe in her own world.

She twisted her body around as much as she could and reached out and pulled the second lump towards her, flipping it over to see if there were symbols written on the soles of the other foot. There were - another three symbols stared back at her, all completely unique and maddeningly indecipherable.

The thought struck her that she could use her powers to unfreeze what was now clearly some sort of machine - very different from Eight in many ways, but also rather similar in others. For one, the polished restless black of the trunk and rootbranches were clearly the same material as Eight, even if Eight was a chunky hunk of solid Tekktate and this was thin, spindly, twisted and complex. She was just about to let the green Kora flow, when she remembered v0-LT-2, and wondered if it had comrades, accomplices or even slave-machines to help do its evil bidding. Maybe this machine that looked so twisted from the outside was also dark and twisted on the inside? But maybe it knew things about this world, and about Time, and about a way home? Maybe it could help? The thought of home trumped all other concerns and made her mind up for her.

'Perhaps if I gave it just enough power to activate it for a minute or so it might be ok,' she thought. 'Then if it turns out to be wicked, it will likely freeze again before it can do anything too bad to me...'

She clambered her way out through the rootbranches and stood once more on the outside of the misshapen tree-like machine. She knew it was an awful risk, but regardless, she extended one finger tentatively and let the briefest shock of green charge escape from her fingertip into the machine.

Suddenly the cavern rang out with great whipping and twanging sounds that reverberated around the large space, as the mass of rootbranches - in an instant - coiled around themselves into a tight and streamlined cylinder.

Kat quickly took several steps back to move out of the way of the rapid (but amazingly elegant) re-coiling of the machine. The whipping and twanging gave way to a loud buzzing sound that made Kat cover her ears. 'No, that's not right,' she thought as she tried to place the new sound. 'Not buzzing, drilling...'

She looked at the space where the tree had been to see it disappear down, down, down into the hole that it had made for itself with its drilling - corkscrewing its way out of sight so rapidly it made Kat gasp. New lumps of Tekktate were thrown from the hole into the air above her, and she watched as they slowed to a halt in the stale air above her - displaced in space and Time by the green-powered physical contact of this machine, then refrozen by the vacuum of no-Time that was all around. Then, again, there was total silence.

From deep down in the hole, there came choral voices.

'Where... are we?' came the first voice.

'How am I supposed to know?' came another.

'What... do you... remember?' asked one more.

'Not much...' said a different voice.

'Why are we... talking like this?' asked another.

'These words... strange, are they not?' came the first voice again.

'Huh...' said the third voice. 'Were we learning... whilst we were asleep? How?'

'We were not just sleeping, sillies,' snorted a new voice. 'Do you not remember - how it became too tough to drill anything. How slowly we moved?'

'That is correct!' said the fifth voice. 'I remember now - we were drilling just as normal and then everything went all slow and red and weird and I just could not stop from drifting into low-power mode.'

'It is right you know,' said another voice. Kat could not make out if it was a voice she had already heard or not. 'It is fuzzy - but I think something may have happened to the world. Things started to change, and we could see it was wrong somehow and then we all started a meeting about what it could be and then we began to unravel and could not stop it and then we all started to drift away, one by one.'

'Fuzzy,' laughed another voice. 'What a funny word.'

'How did you know what this word meant?' asked another.

'We should get out of this hole and look around,' said the first voice, ignoring the last voice that spoke. 'Maybe there is something up there that will explain why we powered up.'

'Good idea,' said one of the voices.

'Great idea,' said another.

'The best idea,' said one more voice.

Kat's head was swimming with all the babbling voices. Even when just one voice spoke its choral quality made it sound as though they were all speaking at the same time. She did not have long to ponder what it all could mean - from deep within the hole there were sounds of mechanical clunking, ratcheting and hissing exertions before an enormous BOING sound erupted from underground and a very tall, thin machine coiled tightly like a huge spring landed in front of her on the two enormous feet she had examined earlier. She looked from its feet all the way up its sleek body to its triangular shaped head that was made of the shiniest and most polished Tekktate she had yet seen, with a long peak so razor-sharp it looked like it could cut through anything. Its head was crossed with the same striations she had felt on the tunnel walls - it had just one small dial for an eye near the centre of its face-plate (slightly off to one side), and just below its dial ran a visible seam that opened up into a thin diagonal slot that could have been a mouth. Kat was unsure if that was its actual purpose - but there it was in any case.

'Hullo,' said the machine, as it slightly bent forward and loomed down over Kat for a closer look at the girl.

'Erm... hi,' said Kat - a little intimidated by its sheer size - but again giving a little wave just as she had done when she met Eight for the first time.

'Did you...?' asked the machine, as it uncoiled several strands to form a crude hand shape and began to mimic Kat's wave.

'Did I... what?' replied Kat.

The machine did not answer, and Kat realised that the tiny shock of green Kora had already run its course. She thought for a few seconds, then slowly walked around the new, super-sleek form of what used to be a distorted mass of rootbranches but was now almost the exact opposite.

'Well...' she thought. 'None of those voices sounded evil or dark or twisted to me - just confused. How strange, though. I'm sure it would be ok to give it a little more power...'

She joined her hand with the frozen hand-like shape of the machine and let a healthy dose of green Kora flow.

'…awaken us?' continued the machine, seemingly unaware that it had briefly frozen again.

'Yes… I did,' she replied. 'I'm Kat,' she continued. 'What are you called?'

'You are a cat?' said one of the voices. 'What is a cat?'

'Not a cat, silly,' said a voice. 'Kat. I think that is the designation of this creature. A cat is a different animal.'

'What is an animal?' asked another voice.

'Huh. I do not know how I know that,' said the voice. The machine bent further over until the sharp tip of its head was almost touching Kat's. 'What have you DONE to us?' it yelled.

Kat took a step back. 'Nothing, honestly!' she pleaded. 'Yes, I woke you up and it seems that when I use my powers somehow some of the things I know are transferred. I don't know how, or why, but I mean you no harm, really. In fact, I could use your help.'

'Powers?' said one of the voices, and Kat began to rapidly explain everything that had happened to her and Artie and Lewis and Eight so far that day. When she was finished, the tall machine straightened again and started talking to itself once more.

'Terrible story. Awful,' said a voice.

'Do we believe it?' asked one of the other voices.

'Her,' corrected another voice. 'Be polite. I believe her.'

'I do too,' said another.

'Me too,' said another.

After a short while all the voices in the machine seemed to agree that Kat was a good thing, whatever the girl-thing was that she was, and that they should probably help her and the boy-things and the other machine.

'I do not like the sound of this v0-LT-2 character,' said the first voice. 'If it is responsible for breaking our world, we must stop it. Otherwise, we will not ever be able to finish our task here!'

'Can I ask...' began Kat, '...what *is* your task here? Why are you digging up this city?'

'Impressive, is it not?' said one of the voices with obvious pride as more of its body uncoiled into arms that then rested where its hips would be - if it had any. Its pointed head turned slowly all the way around as it spoke, just like an owl's does. 'All our own work, this - this cavern, the tunnels, the machinery. We drilled it all, uncovered it all.'

'Yes, very impressive,' said Kat sincerely, looking around too. 'But why?'

'Good question,' said a voice.

'Excellent, wise question,' said another.

'The best question,' said a third pointedly.

Kat waited, then ran out of patience and gestured to the machine for more.

'No idea,' said one of the voices.

'Orders is orders,' said another.

'Dig it up, we were instructed,' said another. 'So we did.'

Kat shook her head, exasperated. For a single machine with so many individual thoughts and voices it did not seem to actually know very much at all. She wondered if this machine was in fact a little bit broken. Regardless, it had vowed to help her, and she had been apart from the boys and Eight for far too long. Anything could be happening above ground and she now felt the irresistible urge to get back to them.

'Can you help me get out of here?' she asked politely. 'My friends are waiting - and they may be in trouble… I have a kind of map - I'm sure I now know the way back to them.'

'No need,' said one of the voices. 'We made this amazing place, we know the quickest way up. We will see you right.'

Kat stared at this utterly bizarre machine who she now rested her hopes on, shaking her head again in disbelief. Still, of all the strange things that had happened to her today, this was nothing to what was yet to come.

CHAPTER EIGHT

Eight meet Five

Lewis screamed in anger and frustration at the ground that had swallowed his sister. He turned to look at Artie, who was deep in thought but otherwise motionless. He looked forlornly at Eight, who was also motionless, and now completely out of power - likely not thinking about anything at all.

'How long has it been?' Lewis asked towards Artie, who finally looked up at his friend before shrugging his shoulders.

'I'm going to try again,' said Lewis indignantly and strode across to the immobile machine, laid his trembling hands on the shiny black exterior and pressed as hard as he could.

Green Kora gently pulsed across Lewis' skin, just below the epidermal layer, but no green charge escaped, and nothing happened to the big hunk of ancient but sleek technology lying beneath his palms.

'Aaarrrggghhh!' he yelled and kicked the ground, before sobs started to leak from him that roused Artie. Lewis turned back towards Eight and initially moved to punch the machine out of sheer frustration - but instead caught himself in the act and laid both palms on the machine to rest.

Artie strode across to his best friend and put one arm around his shoulder, with the other hand rested on the machine like his friend's. It was not much, but Artie felt that some show of solidarity between the three of them was better than nothing right now.

'We'll find her,' he said reassuringly. 'Or she'll find us, more likely. You know Kat. She might be the youngest, but you know she's a whole lot wiser than both of us put together.'

Artie suddenly felt a tingle in his splayed hand and looked down to see the green power visibly coursing through his skin, pulling his hand inch by inch in one direction. He saw that the same thing was happening to Lewis' hand (who was too upset to have noticed yet). Artie watched the strange movements of their hands as they were tugged closer together like some sort of magnet just on the edge of finding an attraction. Their hands lurched closer and closer, then with one final heave, their two palms almost met, and a bolt of bright green charge exploded between the two and arced up into the air and then down into Eight's blackened body.

The servos in Eight's lower head section fired up and its three dials illuminated once more and began to quickly alternate between their settings. It rotated its head back and forth, taking in the sight of the startled boys who were now staring at their hands trying to understand what had just happened.

'My friends,' said Eight. 'I do believe I may have powered down - just for a second.'

Artie let out a small chuckle, and even Lewis, who felt less like he wanted to laugh than he ever had, managed a small smile.

More clunking and whirring and hissing noises escaped Eight's stocky, hunched frame, but the machine did not move.

'Hmmm,' it mused. 'I do not have enough power to operate most of my hydraulics it seems.'

'Then you shouldn't try,' said Artie. 'Trying will probably just use up more power.'

Eight looked around once more. 'Kat is not here,' it stated. 'How was I repowered?'

'We did it,' said Lewis. 'Although... I'm not really sure how.'

'We should try again,' said Artie assertively, and immediately grabbed Lewis' hand. They both, with one hand holding the other's, laid their free hands on Eight's body. The green charge flowed once more, but only for a couple of seconds before it faded completely.

'I think we're pretty much out,' said Lewis solemnly. Artie nodded his head in agreement and his smile turned quickly into a frown. Lewis wondered if any more of the green Kora was refusing to leave their bodies, to continue protecting them from the effects of Time.

Eight noticed the change of behaviour in the boys and sensed their despair.

'No matter,' it said buoyantly. 'My logic circuits feel much better, much sharper - as though a veil has been lifted from them. I can think more clearly now.'

'Great!' said Artie. 'So, what do we do?'

'Hmmm. I will need to think on this for a time in order to fully calculate all the possibilities. I shall enter low-power mode to ensure I have enough energy to complete all the calculations. They will, undoubtedly, be very complex,' said the machine as it became silent and dim once more.

Lewis threw his hands up in exasperation and was about to yell again, but instead simply stared at the wilderness before him. The advent of full daylight had done nothing to help the situation - instead of a dark wilderness full of nothing, he could see a light wilderness full of nothing. He thought of the secret entrance to the farm - a something out of nothing and realised that just because he could not see anything nearby - that did not mean there was nothing there at all.

'I'm going for a walk,' he said huffily to Artie as he grabbed a handful of assorted foodstuffs from the knapsack.

'Don't go far - keep within sight,' Artie urged, but did not try to talk his dejected friend out of an activity that may help his mood.

Artie watched as his best friend, his head low, sluggishly traipsed across the frozen ground. Artie thought that Lewis was more likely just killing time than searching for more holes in the ground whilst their weird travelling companion thought deeply in silence.

'Complex calculations?' Artie sniffed as he looked across the wilderness and to the figure gradually getting smaller. 'There's nothing here to work out. I'll bet the machine wakes up any minute.' Artie lay down on the raw Tekktate and closed his eyes. With his mind clearing, he realised how much he already missed Kat and desperately wanted her back.

*

Artie slowly opened his eyes as he heard the muffled sound of shuffling feet. He was unsure how long he had been asleep, or even if he had truly managed to sleep at all. A dark shape loomed over him, blocking the light from the frozen, small, far away suns and silhouetting the figure so that he could not initially make out who it was.

'The machine's awake,' said Lewis, stretching a hand down towards his friend and hauling him back onto his feet.

Artie rubbed his eyes, clearing them of sleep, and turned to look at Eight, whose dials were again lit, and its head was swivelling back and forth.

'Well?' said Artie, not expecting much.

'Our options are limited...' said the machine - to nobody's surprise, '...but our best chance is for me - to make a bomb.'

Lewis felt a wave of fear mixed with excitement at the prospect. Artie just felt excited.

'Cool!' they both said together.

'But...' continued Artie, '...do you have enough power for that? I thought you needed a lot to make a bomb that could break through Time.'

'That is true,' replied the machine. 'The odds are not in our favour. But they are still the best odds of the limited possibilities open to us currently. However, if the situation changes, I will have to re-enter low-power mode and begin my calculations again.'

'Make the bomb!' said Artie hurriedly.

Eight's head moved very slightly up and down in agreement and once more the little scooper device popped out from an invisible opening and gathered a heaped dose of raw

Tekktate. The movement of the scooper seemed more erratic to Lewis, and it seemed to struggle to initially scrape the surface of the ground. The green power within the machine was clearly very limited and Lewis' heart sank as he realised just how unlikely this plan - their only plan - was to work.

From inside the machine a low rumbling sound grew. It was mixed with some gentle pounding noises, which were then augmented by intermittent sloshing, a layer of screeching and then a blast of white noise like the sound from a hair dryer long past its best. It all sounded like the beginning of a symphony played by an orchestra who were only allowed to use dustbin lids, broken pipes, barbed wire and shattered glass as instruments. Despite the combination of noises not being terribly loud, the boys covered their ears as the screeching, clattering sounds went right through them and set their teeth on edge.

A rattling, then a low rumbling sound followed - very similar in tone to the noises in a bowling alley when the ball is returned. A small hatch opened, again seemingly from nowhere, near the base of Eight's body. There was an elongated hiss and then a perfectly round, highly polished but small black sphere dropped onto the ground with a thud.

'You must be quick and move to a safe distance, boys,' said Eight. 'I do not have enough power to move but the bomb will not affect me negatively when it explodes.'

The two boys nodded and scrambled away as fast as they could, sliding onto the ground like pro-baseball players when they had reached a safe distance, and covering their ears whilst still ensuring they had the best view. They stared in anticipation of the pending explosive event and held their breaths.

'ₚₒₚ,' went the bomb, barely audible. Eight's hulky machine torso hardly wobbled from the pathetic blast.

'Hmmm,' said the machine looking down towards the ground. 'Disappointing.'

Artie would have laughed had he not felt so crushed that the chance of finding a way to Kat had amounted to nothing. He did not have long to dwell on this, however, as a low rumbling sound began, and the ground once more began to shake violently.

'Timequake!' gasped Lewis and braced himself for another jolt.

Artie turned and looked towards where the rumbling was coming from and saw a disturbance tear across the ground. This time, however, it was not a rip or crack like the sinkhole that eventually consumed Kat, but multiple mounds of Tekktate being pushed upwards, snaking their way towards the group - coming closer and closer.

Lewis, who had, (when a little younger), always found solace in the slapstick humour of classic cartoons, half-expected the wascally wabbit Bugs Bunny to pop up from the head of the disturbance and ask for directions to Albuquerque. Something did emerge though - a polished black, very sharply pointed triangular shape that was then followed by a long, thin corkscrewed cylinder - part of which unfolded into something that looked branchlike, and which soon resembled an arm, wrist and a hand. It extended its new appendage down into the ground and pulled.

'KAT!' Lewis and Artie exclaimed together as she was hauled up through the newly formed tunnel by the intimidatingly tall machine. The boys rushed over to her and smothered her with hugs and cuddles and kisses. A tear ran from Lewis' eye and he smeared it all over her cheek, but she did not notice as she hugged her brother tighter than she ever had before.

'This is…' she began before realising that the machine never actually got around to introducing itself. 'Oh,' she said. 'This is…' and gestured to the machine to announce itself.

'Our designation is Squaxx-Gruk-Taktak-Huop-Krim-Kuttak,' it said very matter-of-fact and somewhat proudly. Very pleased to meet you all,' one of its voices said.

'What?' said Artie.

'*Our* designation?' asked Lewis, confused.

'In your language, it is designated 5P-R1-N6,' translated Eight.

'Ah, yes,' said the tall machine absent-mindedly. 'We know these characters, somehow. Perhaps we should have spoken in your language. That would have made more sense.'

'We?' asked Lewis again, still confused.

Kat explained all that had happened underground and how, for some reason, this new machine had many, many voices - and the boys formally introduced themselves and Eight.

'Well, it certainly makes things easier for us anyway,' said Artie gesturing between the two machines. 'Eight, meet Five.'

'I like it!' said Five.

'*Do* we like it, really?' said another part of Five, less convinced by their new nickname.

'Sure we do!' said another.

'I prefer Squaxx,' said another. 'More elegant.'

'You would…' said one more voice.

'Well. This is all very… jovial,' said Eight rather grumpily. 'But I remain somewhat - stuck. Perhaps Kat may be so good as to assist me once more?'

Kat walked over to Eight and laid her hands on its chunky body.

'Maybe next time we won't wait so long, huh?' she asked the machine wryly. Eight bowed its head in the same sheepish manner that it seemed to be getting used to doing.

'Yes…' it said. 'The boys are indeed correct. You really are quite sensible and very aware for such a young thing.'

Kat's hands remained on Eight for quite some time, yet the machine seemed concerned by the activity.

'What's wrong?' she asked.

'I am not sure. The green Kora seems to be flowing more slowly into my power-banks than previously. There seems to be some sort of… resistance. Perhaps it is just a temporary anomaly - a blockage of some sort that will clear in time. Pay it no mind.'

Eight quickly changed the subject as it saw the worried expression form more deeply across Kat's face, and addressed the group all together.

'It is possible that our new acquaintance, Five, may be suffering from what we Fabrakkans call simultaneous-ancestral-awakening-syndrome. It is a very, very rare bug - I was under the impression that it had been wiped out many generational upgrades ago. Essentially, all of Five's Maker's chipsets are active at the same time. There is not one dominant chipset - as there should be - they all share the physical functions of the machine together. It is, in essence, a family.'

'I'm not sure I follow, exactly,' said Lewis, screwing his face up.

'Imagine if you, your parents, your grandparents and their parents all existed in the same body all at the same time and all had an opinion about everything,' explained Artie who had understood perfectly.

'Ah,' said Lewis. 'Oh. Eww,' he groaned, pulling a face at the thought of grandma Joan with her whiskery kisses inhabiting his body. As much as he loved her, his body (that was thankfully only his), still shuddered.

Artie looked to the horizon, again searching for some hope of this great city that had been promised.

'Should we be getting on?' he said. 'There's still no sign of this city.'

'Yes, we should,' responded Eight as its hidden hydraulics kicked in and it finally began to move with much hissing and clunking. The group assembled and began to follow Eight's lead and they set off, once more, towards the blank horizon.

'Oh, the city,' said Five gleefully. 'It has been such a long time since we were last there. Wonder what it is like now?'

'How long have you been away?' asked Kat.

'Good question,' said one of Five's voices.

'Excellent question,' said another.

'Yes, yes,' said Kat impatiently, who already knew where this conversation with Five was leading. 'How long?'

'Oh, hundreds of cycles,' replied Five.

'Hundreds and hundreds,' said another Five.

'It takes a long time to excavate a city,' said a different Five. 'It is expert work.'

'Not work for a novice,' said a Five.

'Absolutely not. Experts only,' said another Five.

'So, you know nothing about v0-LT-2 and what happened to the world?' asked Lewis, again feeling a tinge of anxiety at the name.

'Zero,' said Kat who felt the same unpleasant tinge. 'v0-LT-2 is such another mouthful. Let's just call it Zero. Maybe that will help it seem... less threatening somehow.'

The group nodded in agreement at Kat's sensible suggestion. Lewis (although his head nodded along with the others), did not think it made Zero less threatening at all. He shivered, imagining an enormous brute of a machine; as tall as Five, taller perhaps, and as bulky as Eight with nothing but sharp edges and weaponised appendages - probably six, or ten or more arms each with a different sharpened gadget or blaster-cannon or reconfigurable hand that could become a sword to spear you with, then in a split-second a shield to block or deflect any form of attack. He imagined a machine so wicked, so corrupted and so determined to complete its evil plan, that it could not be reasoned with or pleaded with. He gulped and tried to put all thoughts of the evil they may soon have to face out of his head.

Five meanwhile, was quiet, and now appeared to be thinking - which, for a machine with umpteen brains, took quite a while to organise its thoughts.

'Well…' it finally resumed as the group marched on. 'Not nothing exactly. We were visited at the site, on occasion by our supervisor, Twonkle-Kru… sorry - we mean, J0-8WR-7H. We were not always on our own, you see. The last visit was not that long before the world slowed and froze. And it told rumours of strange and sudden happenings in the city. Groups of machines displaying odd behaviours… meeting in the shadows, parts of facilities being closed down and blocked off, barriers being quickly erected. Fabrakka has always been a completely open, free world. The sudden erection of barriers was very unusual. Our supervisor was also concerned that it was being misled… important details about our work being kept hidden, questions not being answered when asked. But… it had no evidence that really anything was actually wrong… just an… what is the word?'

'Feeling?' asked Kat.

'No,' replied Five. 'We do not know that word.'

'Intuition?' asked Artie.

'Yes. That is the one!' said another Five.

Kat stared at the imposingly tall, thin machine before looking at her own hands, confused. Why was it that when she transferred green Kora to the machines, seemingly random information leaked from her? How could Five not know a common word such as *feeling* but did know a far less common word like *intuition*? It either meant nothing at all, and was totally random, or there was something in the Kora that directed it. Perhaps what was transferred was related to what she was herself thinking and feeling at the time... or perhaps the Kora itself decided what to let loose? After all, the machine in the mansion possibly chose her, according to Eight. But Eight was conjecturing - it had no more knowledge of this type of power than she did.

'Do you think that these secretive machines... were followers of Zero?' asked Artie.

'There is insufficient evidence to support that supposition,' said Eight rigidly, before softening. 'But it is a distinct possibility. We must refrain from speculating too much for fear of leading ourselves down the wrong path. We must, however, also remain open to all available options.'

Artie sneered at Eight's slightly contradictory statements. 'But if you had to guess?' he said.

Eight let out a small blast of steam before replying.

'I have previously stated that I am not one for guessing. But I will play your game, Artie. Yes, I do believe that these incidents are linked; Fabrakka did not move in an instant from a world of peace and harmony to a secretive and deceptive one naturally or by simple accident. The likelihood is that one machine has directed this chaos deliberately, and along the way corrupted other, less evolved machines to help achieve its goals. My preliminary calculations show that we are travelling to a city that is now very likely under the direct control of a highly organised group of machines, who may even be immune from the effects of Time.'

'How does a frozen world benefit any machine?' asked Kat. 'What are they trying to achieve?'

Eight extended its internal pistons and lengthened its stride, turning towards Kat as it did so.

'That, my girl - is indeed the question and one we will only be able to answer through investigation. Look!'

Eight pointed to the horizon. A spire had emerged over the crest and was now just visible. Kat had to squint to see it, but it was unmistakable - a dark point in the sky, menacingly silhouetted.

'Is that...?' she asked.

'It is,' interrupted Eight. 'The very centre of the city - the control tower. It is there we are most likely to find the answers we need.'

Eight again lengthened its stride further, and Five copied the other machine to match its speed. The children now had to jog to keep up, but their eyes were all now fixed on the dark spindle on the horizon that with every hurried step grew taller, clearer and more imposing.

CHAPTER NINE

Time Flies

Lewis gulped.

'We have to cross... *that*?' he asked, fearfully.

The group had descended into a vast basin - a short descent of only 30 metres or so, but one that they could not detect until they were almost on top of it. The wide, natural bowl lay below the horizon, and with their eyes fixed firmly on the growing spire of the control tower, the raging contents within it came as quite the surprise.

Eight looked left across the basin, unable to see its full extents. The machine then looked right and found that it was the same. Within the bowl, the sea was so densely bright red that the group found it hard to look directly at. The sea raged more ferociously and climbed far higher than the relatively calm thin seas of red they had experienced so far. Kat knew why, exactly.

'Green,' she said, pointing and peering into the ocean of power. 'There are scattered pools and streams of intense green charge weaving through the red, reacting furiously to it, angering it.' Kat thought back to the small pool of dense green power in the tunnel that was fighting its own personal war with the red charge that surrounded it. This was exactly the same, but on a far, far larger scale. The water-fountain-like arcs here were gigantic, arcing much higher even than Five. These were not at all playful, she thought - more like huge snaking walls of fiery death. And every few seconds, from the surface of the sea, towering bolts of green or red energy shot up into the sky, like great valves releasing pressure. If Fabrakka had any bird-like machines soaring over the ocean, immune to the effects of Time, they would have been clobbered by these upward blasts of energy.

'Perhaps my dials need an upgrade,' Eight said as its lens frantically zoomed in and out. 'I cannot see where this basin ends. There is too much disturbance caused by the Kora - the extents of this feature are undetectable. To find a way around, rather than across, may take an inordinate amount of time.'

Artie sighed but, as usual, grabbed the bull by the horns. 'Across we go, then. There must be a path across... somehow.'

Just then a large wave of red swelled past in front of the group, chased by a stream of green. The edges of both raged violently at one another, but between them - just like in the tunnel pool - there was a gap; a buffer of nothing.

'Look,' said Artie, his hand outstretched. 'See there? That gap. Do you think...'

Kat, Lewis, Eight and Five turned towards him, each displaying their own look of incredulity on their faces and face-plates. One by one their expressions softened or dimmed, as they realised Artie's ridiculous suggestion was in fact their only real option.

'We must try to move swiftly and keep to the gaps between the Kora,' shouted Eight as they began, plunging into the nearest gap in the ocean. The machine had to raise its voice to be heard over the fiery, crackling sparks that were now all around them. 'Any significant contact with the red charge will likely drain Five and I very quickly - and it is possible that the green charge, in these highly dense concentrations - may have unforeseen effects. It may even overload us.'

'And then we really will be in a pickle,' said Lewis offhand, and mostly to himself.

Eight heard the boy's throwaway comment - and studied him whilst also attempting to keep its concentration on the weaving gaps, whose edges sparked in its face-plate and made it very difficult to keep track of the constantly shifting movements.

'I do not see how the preservation of foodstuffs via a largely acidic solution is relevant at this precise moment,' said Eight. Lewis thought that it was mechanically wheezing as it scolded him - perhaps the pace of the group was too much for the hunched machine? This contraption did seem to be becoming more and more run-down inside with each new incident the group encountered.

Eight stopped abruptly and threw out its heavy arms to either side, just like a lollipop-person would do in defiance of a particularly lax driver at a crossing. An enormous wave of red swelled past in front of the group, and the gap they were aiming for disappeared before their very eyes and dials. The group turned and looked all around them - they were trapped in a circular buffer with huge walls of red charge raging around them, circling them menacingly.

Kat felt something. At first, she was not sure what it was, but then the feeling grew and grew. She sensed the red Kora, circling them ominously, was studying them - trying to figure them out. Was that even possible? And was it just her imagination - or was the buffer now shrinking?

'Erm... what do we do?' asked Lewis, his voice breaking nervously as it became clear the buffer was indeed getting smaller and smaller.

'This has become quite the day,' said Five.

'Like no other,' said another Five.

'Perhaps we should...' began another Five, but it did not complete its sentence as a wave of the brightest green charge crashed through the edge of the buffer in front of them, displacing the edge of the red and creating a new free channel ahead.

'Quick! Now!' yelled Artie, and the group dashed along the newly formed tunnel of nothing. Lewis looked behind him as they burst forward into a new temporary haven to see the buffer behind smashed to nothing as another wave consumed it. He heard a ratcheting sound as Five extended its legs to again lengthen its stride. The machine, in this adjusted configuration, danced quickly forward like a boxer as light on its toes as possible - readying to spar with the immense ocean. This eclectic party of children and machines now moved as one, each in their own unique style, trying to anticipate the swell of the warring red and green powers and weave into and through the gaps as they appeared and lurched and bent without warning. It was exhausting, and despite all their efforts, none of the group could work out how much progress they had made - moving through the sea was like trying to nail down jelly.

After an exhausting few minutes, with the group panting hard and struggling for breath, or hissing with steam from every invisible opening in their cases, the seas calmed a little, then they calmed a lot. The gap they were in was comfortably large and was not shifting very much at all - just gently swaying at the edges.

'Strange,' mused Eight. 'I could be mistaken, but I believe we may have reached the middle of the sea.'

'Ah…' said Artie, clutching his side trying to stop the full effects of a stitch forming, '…like the eye of… a storm. Calm in the middle… but raging all around… the edges?'

'Precisely,' said Eight.

'Indubitably,' said Five, who seemed to have found yet another amusing new word somewhere deep in its database that it was keen to try out.

'Yes… well…' continued Eight. 'Perhaps we should take advantage of this fortunate serenity and briefly rest. I suggest the children snack on something from their knapsacks?'

The children all hungrily nodded in agreement and Artie delved into his knapsack and started handing out oranges, apples and assorted nuts. Within just a few short moments they had eaten fully and that was just as well, as Five spoke up with renewed haste.

'We think the calm may be coming to an end,' it said, uncoiling itself into a pointed arm and hand that gestured towards the edges of the gap. The wall had started to move again inwards and spark more intensely.

'We should be off,' said a different Five.

'Without delay,' said another.

'Right awa…' began another.

'Stop yammering and start running!' yelled Artie as a swell of red crashed into the buffer, narrowly missing the group and cutting their safe haven in half. The group started at speed but had to change direction almost instantly as a torrent of green sliced through without warning - and fully consumed Lewis.

'Lew…!' yelled Artie - but there was no sign of him - he had completely vanished.

*

Lewis opened his eyes and looked down at his hands. Everything was oddly swimming, just as if he was underwater, and his own skin was a shimmering emerald colour. He looked beyond the wobbling green wall of energy and turned to where the group had been, just a second ago.

'Thank goodness,' he said as he saw the group just a handful of metres away. As he looked closer, he realised that something did not seem quite right. He took a step closer to them - they were not moving at all… they were completely still.

'Artie?' he queried, before yelling 'KAT!' as loudly as he could. The group did not respond at all - neither Artie nor Kat even blinked. He waved his hands furiously to make himself seen - he was only a couple of metres away from them and yet there was still no reaction. He turned all the way around - a full 360 degrees - and it dawned on him that he was surrounded by green Kora in every direction. In fact, he was inside it.

Lewis edged closer to the towering circular wall of green that separated him from his friends. He extended his hand and tried to push it into the sparking green barrier. It shoved him back so violently he landed on his bottom a full three metres back.

'Ow,' he said, rubbing his smarting behind as he tried to stand up.

'OW!' he yelled, again, more strongly - as a sharp pain, like a hot knife, split his temple. He instinctively laid his palm on the side of his head in an attempt to ease the pressure and the pain, but it had little effect. His head was now throbbing and thumping hard - and his mind began to race. Thought after thought flooded his brain - he replayed the entire day's events over in his mind in just a few seconds and found himself suddenly back at home with his parents then at school that day of the surprise test he was not prepared for and then back at the farm then that almost-fight with Lloyd that he had run away from then apologising to his teacher for forgetting his homework then helping his dad by handing him his tools as he worked on the old car. Thoughts and memories tumbled over themselves and Lewis' head could not handle it, and everything went dark as he fell to the ground.

When he awoke it was dark which made him very confused. And he was starving! His headache had lessened a little - it still throbbed but the searing pains had gone. Why was he so hungry? He had eaten only a few moments ago when the group rested, and he could not have been out for very long. But then why was it dark? *How* could it be dark? Had there been another Timequake when he was unconscious?

He sat up and looked around. Everything still looked wobbly and green, although it was a very dark green which made it even harder to see anything clearly. He looked for the group, and saw them, still in exactly the same place and still completely frozen. He studied the edges of the furiously sparking wall of energy again - how was he ever going to get out of this? As he looked, he realised that it was becoming rapidly lighter again. His hunger pangs kicked in ferociously and he returned to his knapsack and pulled out some food. The nuts were fine, and still plentiful and he devoured a handful. The apples and oranges and berries, however, had changed. Their skins had begun to wrinkle, and sag, and they no longer felt firm the way deliciously ripe fruit did. He realised that they would not last and so ate more of them than he needed - whilst he still could.

He looked around again to see that it was already completely light, just like it is in the very middle part of the day. As he looked over to the frozen group, he could see them dim and fade as the darkness quickly swallowed them once more - a full Fabrakkan day had passed in just a few moments. His head hurt once more, but he forced himself towards the wall and again tried to push into the barrier to free himself of this prison. The wall sparked so furiously he flew even further back with the blast than he had last time. Sore and once again, suddenly, incredibly tired - he did not even attempt to get back to his feet and instead fell into another troubled sleep.

Hunger woke him, and before he had even fully opened his eyes he was fumbling and searching in his knapsack for more food. The berries and apples were even more wrinkled now, and had split, but he did not have the luxury of fussiness and so ate them without a pause. The sourness shocked his tongue and he forced the distasteful morsels down his throat, swallowing hard. He gasped and panted as he realised how thirsty he now was, and it was only then that he twigged he had absolutely no water with him. His heart sank and the same horrible feeling in the pit of his stomach he had had that day of the surprise test hit him hard, but more extremely. Trapped in this prison, with no help of rescue from his petrified friends, with limited food and no water he understood for the first time that he really could die here.

He began to panic and rushed across to the wall to where, just beyond reach, his friends stood motionless. His first instinct was to bang hard on the barrier - but what good would that do? It was not a solid object - no noise could be made by hitting it, nor would they be able to hear him in any case. He could not force the wall down through any show of strength and he really did not fancy another shock that propelled him high into the air followed by another painful, bruising landing.

He slumped to the ground, defeated, and lay on his back and looked upwards. Time rushed past; dark became light became dark and he wished he could see the stars to study and take his mind off his predicament, but the wobbly green energy made it too difficult to see. He was not even sure the stars were there. He stared into space and absentmindedly reached into his knapsack for an orange, but instead his fingers found something else; the professor's notebook, that he had completely forgotten about.

He sat up, intrigued, and began to flick through the pages. He was not sure, initially, what sort of book it was. Was it a diary or journal of some kind? Was it a scientific notebook, full of equations and diagrams? Was it even a guide to Fabrakka based on the professor's observations?

As he thumbed through, he soon discovered that it was some of all of these things. Some pages did indeed have schematics for new inventions and machines - including some parts which clearly ended up being used in the mashed potato machines. Some pages were filled with unrecognisable symbols - were these parts of a scientific language he was too young to know - or perhaps they were even the Fabrakkan language, (one of the symbols did look vaguely familiar)? If the professor had studied and learnt their language did that mean he had interacted with some of the machines? When? Who?

He flicked through some more pages - many of them had annotations alongside the diagrams about a new idea or a correction of something the professor had tried but had clearly not worked out as he had hoped. Some pages had basic observations about the raw materials including some rather poetic descriptions about Tekktate that soon descended into an incandescent scrawling rage as the professor struggled to understand how the blackened, indestructible but oily material could possibly even exist. Lewis noticed that the further he progressed through the pages, the more erratic the handwriting became. The language changed too - sentences became shorter and more abrupt, and the use of exclamation marks increased. Several pages had been crossed out entirely and scored through and some pages were ripped as though the professor had written with such fury his pen had torn right through the paper. Lewis could sense the increasing frustration and desperation leap from the pages as he worked his way from cover to cover. On one of the final pages, however, everything changed. An elegant and neat diagram, almost without any supporting annotation, stared back from the page and Lewis recognised it as the machine from the room in the mansion that brought them to Fabrakka. At the bottom of the page was written just one word, in capital letters - SUCCESS!!! - and this was underlined numerous times. Lewis turned the remaining pages to see that they were all blank. What did this mean? Did the professor find a way to return home? If that was so, where is he now? Why was there no further trace of him in Lewis' own world? And did this mean that there was another identical machine, somewhere on Fabrakka, that could take them home?

Lewis' heart raced and pounded excitedly at the thought and then he looked at the walls of his green prison and realised that it all meant nothing.

*

'...is!' yelled Artie.

Kat looked around, panicked, for her brother - but could not see any trace. The green had taken him.

Suddenly, she was flattened by a thin form that emerged from nowhere and collapsed on top of her. It was a very bushy creature, bedraggled and gaunt, gasping and croaking and drooling in her face.

'Get off me!' she yelled and struggled and rolled the hairy creature away from her.

Artie hauled her back to her feet and stood protectively in front of her as he then bent down to prod the shaggy mess that was now lying on its front. It did not move, and Artie tentatively rolled it over, revealing the knapsack that was lying underneath its body.

'Lewis?' he queried, lacking any understanding of how this could be.

'Wa... wa... ter,' Lewis croaked, desperately.

Artie nodded and turned to Eight, who was already in the process of concocting and purifying more water in its noisy innards that had again begun to bubble and slosh. Artie grabbed the droplet when it was ready and placed it gently on Lewis' mouth whilst cupping the nape of his neck to help him to drink. Lewis drank it down, then exhaustedly fell asleep.

'How… how is…?' began Kat, as she rummaged in the knapsack, now completely empty of everything except the tatty notebook.

'Time,' said Eight matter-of-fact, as the machine studied Lewis closely, whirring and clunking. 'Look at his hair, his fingernails - they have grown immensely. Observe how thin he is - he has been without food or water for days. More, most probably.'

'But he was gone for about two seconds!' she cried, still not fully grasping it.

'He has been inside the green,' said Eight. 'Completely enveloped by it. Time must have been moving at a very different pace to that which we experienced. That would explain why he simply vanished to our dials, and to him, we may have appeared entirely frozen - perhaps for weeks on end…' The machine stopped talking, rather suddenly, but its innards clunked even more loudly as it thought hard and its servos buzzed as it spun its head around.

'This route is too dangerous. I do not believe we can continue this way. There is a great chance that one of us, or more, could become lost forever. It would appear that Lewis has been very lucky.'

'Lucky?' replied Kat, indignantly as she stared down at the brother she now barely recognised. She expected one of the machines to continue talking but neither of them did for a time.

'We do not recognise this world,' said Five.

'No, it is very different to the one we left to go underground and begin our task,' said another Five.

'So entirely different,' said another Five, ponderously.

'Underground...' said Artie as he stared into the now seemingly uncrossable ocean. 'That's it! We go underground and pass the sea that way!'

'Great suggestion,' said Five. 'We can help with that!'

'No problem at all,' said another Five.

'We really should have suggested that all along,' said a different Five.

Kat stared forlornly at the tall machine as though to say, 'please don't let that be true.' A wall of red swelled dangerously close and Kat's expression hardened until Five finally grasped her meaning and began to drill.

CHAPTER TEN

The Great Machine City

'Hwmwfmwmfwllmlllmmff?' came a muffled sound from deep within the hole.

'Pardon?' said Kat, straining to understand or hear over the noise of drilling.

Five extracted its sharp, pointed head from the new tunnel it had begun to drill and tried again. 'How is Lewis now?' it called down the ever-lengthening passageway.

She looked at the machine and felt an almost irrepressible urge to reprimand him for drilling with its mouth full, just as her mother had often done to her when she tried to eat and talk at the same time. Her brother lay, resting on the hard ground, thinner and weaker than she had ever seen him and her heart ached at the dishevelled sight. She and Artie had carried him underground and then part of the way along the new tunnel that Five had drilled. That had, however, become more like dragging - as he was still, oddly, quite heavy - much heavier than he looked.

'He seems... more content,' she replied. 'Thanks for asking,' she quickly added, trying to remain polite to the machine who was, after all, showing genuine concern. Lewis had been twitching and lurching whilst unconscious, although that seemed to have mostly ceased - for now.

Five nodded then resumed its drilling, although to Kat, the noise seemed different than before. Artie noticed too and quietly sidled over to where she stood.

'Is it just me, or is it slowing down?' he whispered in her ear.

'No,' she whispered back, with one eye on the machine deep in the dark tunnel drilling away. 'It's not just you.'

After Five had drilled down deep enough that they felt they were safe from the raging seas above ground, the two machines had debated how best to proceed. Eight had marched off on its own and studied, in annoyingly slow ('thorough') detail, the density and composition of the Tekktate in this area and concluded that blasting would be a little more effective, but Five, Five and a whole host of other Fives all thought that blasting would still be too dangerous for the children. Eight conceded that the Fives were of course correct, and safety was the better option - especially given the torrent of danger above they had just escaped. Progress, however, was slow - and getting slower.

'Maybe the machine needs a boost of green power?' asked Artie. 'Who knows how much all those personalities inside drain it…'

Kat nodded and approached the entrance to the new tunnel and called along it.

'Five?' she hollered, then waited. The sound of drilling had stopped, but then there was no reply as expected. 'Five?' she called out again.

After a few moments of silence, she clambered up into the tunnel and made her way along the darkness. The red in this area was very thin and dim making it hard, yet again, to see much at all. 'Perhaps we have gone too deep underground,' she wondered to herself. 'It was a very long way down, but better to be safe than…'

She bumped into the machine, which was completely motionless, confirming that it had indeed run out of the green charge.

Tutting to herself, she laid her hands on the machine and let the green flow. A tiny charge of green sparked from her hands, and then - nothing.

'Oh no,' she thought and tried again, but no Kora came from within her body. She ran back along the tunnel calling out to Artie and Eight, who met the breathless girl at the entrance.

'It's out! And so am I!' she cried, presenting her useless hands. Artie offered her his own hand and helped her climb down from the elevated tunnel entrance.

'Let me try,' he said, clambering into the tunnel and disappearing into the dark.

Eight turned to Kat, shaking its head. 'This will not work,' it said morosely. Artie soon re-emerged from the tunnel, also shaking his head.

'How much power do you have, Eight?' Artie asked - somewhat fearing the answer.

'Little,' it replied. 'The resistance I felt when Kat attempted to repower me previously has grown inside me, for a reason I cannot detect. I can feel that it is now draining me at an increasingly rapid rate. Our situation... is not an ideal one.'

'At least we aren't being swallowed up by raging waves...' Artie said, trying to look on the bright side.

'Of course!' said Kat. 'Lewis! What if Lewis absorbed some of the green Kora?'

The group turned to look at the thin, hairy boy lying curled up on the ground, finally at some brief peace.

'We must wake him,' said Eight.

'I know,' said Kat, feeling sorry for her exhausted brother who surely needed a lot more, and far more comfortable rest than he was currently enjoying.

Kat leaned over Lewis and began to gently stroke his hair hoping it would be enough to rouse him. It was not quite enough - he grumbled and rolled over - so she began to gently shake him. Again, he moved, trying to nudge away whatever the annoying thing was, and Kat sighed and removed her hands - reluctant to disturb him further.

'Oi! Wake up!' Artie yelled, kicking Lewis' foot hard, but in the manner that only best friends can get away with.

Lewis sat bolt upright and yelled 'Professor?' before rubbing his eyes and seeing the blurry shapes become his twin sister, his best friend and a set of dimly lit dials floating in the darkness.

'Oh,' he said with relief - as it all came flooding back. He looked around, further relieved to see that everything was not swimming and green and sparking in his face.

'How are you feeling?' asked Kat with genuine concern.

'What was it like?' asked Artie, desperate to know more of his adventure inside the raw power of the world.

'How did you manage to facilitate your withdrawal from the Kora?' asked Eight, before realising and correcting itself. 'Apologies. How did you escape?'

Lewis sighed. 'I feel tired. And sore. And it was intense and oddly painful. And exhausting. And I waited until there was a sort of lull - a space in the barrier of green power where it finally calmed. It felt like a very, very long time. Even sometimes where it looked calmer, it wasn't really, and I got another shock when I tried to escape. How long was I gone?'

'2.14968 seconds,' said Eight.

Lewis stared at the blackened machine in the darkness that was still mostly just floating dials to his weakened, unadjusted eyes.

'No really?' he asked - then saw that both Kat and Artie were nodding. He sighed. 'But I went days and days without water! A week at least without food. I mean, I dunno. The suns rose and set more times than I could count, and...'

'We need your help,' interrupted the machine.

'Badly,' said Artie. 'Come on - up you get,' he continued, hauling Lewis onto his feet. 'You don't feel as though you went weeks without food,' he panted, struggling with the effort.

After a few minutes of difficult walking - Lewis was still quite unsteady on his feet - they reached the immobile machine at the end of the tunnel. Five's pointed head was still partly stuck into the Tekktate, frozen mid-drill.

'You should probably stand back,' said Lewis who grimaced and winced as he moved to lay his hands on the coiled exterior of Five.

'Take care not to overload it,' cautioned Eight.

Artie took a few steps back, fearing that when Five reactivated, it would immediately resume the messy, noisy job of drilling, throwing out Tekktate in all directions.

Lewis, feeling somewhat unsure of himself, made hesitant contact with Five. Bursts of green instantly flew everywhere, bouncing and arcing off every surface of the machine, the tunnel and himself in blinding flashes of light that made the children cover and close their eyes tight.

When the light eventually dimmed and the children tentatively opened their eyes again, they could see the tunnel - but no Five. After a few seconds, the drilling noise - which was surprisingly muted and far away - ceased.

'Whooweee-eee!' came a voice far, far down the dark tunnel.

'That was incredible!' said another voice.

'Best ride ever!' said another.

'The power! Can we do that again?' asked another.

Lewis looked down at his hands.

Artie grabbed one and looked closely at it, still pulsing with the residual effects of the Kora. 'Well, I guess that answers one question. You definitely have plenty green in you!'

'That's an understatement!' said Lewis, who had now started to feel much more like himself.

Artie gestured to Kat and Eight to come closer, and then put his hands on his best friend's shoulders and gave them a shake. 'Attaboy,' he said, and the group proceeded to follow the route the tall machine had made for them, still hollering and whooping as it drilled faster, deeper and longer than it ever had before.

Down in the underground, they had forgotten the enormous distance they still had to cover, and with no spire to guide them the journey still felt slow. Lewis had regaled them with the tale of his time in the green, the notes he had read from the professor's notebook, and one more thing that he had not realised until he had to say it out loud.

'I might have been trapped, and unable to find a way out without being hurt... but during all of it - I had this nagging feeling... like... like...' He struggled for the words that best described what he felt.

'Like?' asked Kat.

'Like the green Kora was protecting me somehow. Looking out for me.'

Kat nodded and knew exactly what he meant.

Five was far out of sight, and even the sound of its drilling was very muffled and distant - although the children questioned if that was also due to the fact that the noise had to travel through (or around) a vacuum of no-Time to reach them. Lewis, whose interest in the Kora had now been piqued, wondered how it all worked - when Time came into contact with the green power it was clearly freed from its bounds, but for how long? When the green-powered Five moved through a tunnel - did the Time there slow and dissipate, or was it binary - just on or off? Kat, Artie and Lewis had all run so low on power at some point that they could not restart the machines, but they did not feel Time start to affect them - to slow them. What if they had simply waited - would

Time eventually catch up with their Kora-free bodies and freeze them to the spot, as it had done Eight and Five? Lewis shivered at the thought but was shaken out of it by the distant call of Five.

'Erm... we have a problem!' it called back down the tunnel.

The group upped their pace to catch up with the driller who was still quite far ahead of them. When they reached it, they saw a rather unusual sight. Instead of drilling, the machine was standing upright - although partly coiled over, as the tunnel was nowhere near as high as it was long, and Five was a very tall machine. Five was banging its head repeatedly against the wall of the tunnel.

'Finally gone mad,' whispered Artie to Kat. 'It was only a matter of time.'

'Cannot - BANG - drill - BANG - through - BANG - here - BANG.'

'No - BANG - siree - BANG.'

'That is quite enough of that,' said Eight, urging Five to stop, which it did. 'Are you already low on power?'

'No,' replied Five. 'Plenty of power. We feel great!'

'Hmmm,' mused Eight as it moved closer to the end of the tunnel and stood facing the blackened wall. Suddenly, a multitude of previously invisible flaps, hatches and holes opened in Eight and tools of every description sprung forward - tapping, sweeping, prodding, pounding and scanning the Tekktate all around.

'Hmmm,' mused Eight again, who then turned its attention to Five's drill-tipped head and continued to tap, prod, sweep and scan the machine with its impressive swiss-army-knife toolkit.

'Rarely have I ever encountered Tekktate of this density. In fact...' Eight whirred and clunked again as it searched its databanks, '...I never have. This form of Tekktate is completely unique!'

Kat thought she detected an element of childlike glee in the machine's tone, as though it had uncovered some amazing hidden treasure. Eight noisily moved all around the end of the tunnel still scanning, then worked its way back down the tunnel, pausing more frequently for longer, deeper scans.

'Beyond this tunnel, in every direction, the Tekktate grows denser and denser. It is possible that we have found the limits of what our friend here can drill through.'

'Preposterous!' retorted Five.

'Impossible' said another Five.

'Never have we been so insulted!' said another.

'The round machine is probably correct,' countered a different Five, which sparked a furious argument with itself that went on for minutes.

'Enough!' yelled Artie tugging at his own hair. 'Is Eight correct? Are we stuck - AGAIN?'

Five harrumphed mechanically.

'Yes,' it sighed. 'This has never happened before. We have never found anything we could not drill through.'

'Sad times,' said one of the Fives, gloomily.

'We are not as perfect as we thought,' said a different Five.

'Speak for yourself,' said another. 'I was pretty close, but then you had to go and replace my amazing X698Y-motor with an inferior next-generation upgrade. I said it was the wrong choice at the time, did I not?' Another furious argument erupted, and the children and Eight retreated to a quieter part of the tunnel, leaving the machine to squabble with itself.

'What do we do?' asked Artie.

Eight whirred and turned to Lewis. 'We may have to blast,' said Eight, a little excitedly. 'I observed the impressive effect you had on Five when you recharged it. My preliminary calculations show that a similar effect on my own innards may produce a bomb that could disrupt Tekktate even at this density. Look at the tunnels, children. Notice that the red Kora is so very thin this far down, as though the effects of Time are much weaker. I calculate that it may be possible to blast through.'

'It's worth a shot,' said Artie.

'But, it's dangerous...' said Lewis.

Eight nodded. 'It is, but the tunnels provide perfect cover. Five could, back there where it is less dense, drill a small enough alcove that will protect you all. There is risk, but my analysis is that there is less risk than returning and attempting to re-cross the ocean.'

'...AND WHAT *ABOUT* MY REVISED SCHEMATIC FOR THE RECOILING MECHANISM?' came an angry yell from down the tunnel. 'WORK OF GENIUS THAT WAS!'

'It's still going at it...' sighed Lewis.

'Leave this to me,' said Eight and marched off down the tunnel into the darkness, its internal pistons hissing in determined strides. A short time later, a sheepish-looking Five emerged followed by a stern-looking Eight.

'Good plan,' said Five, who had clearly been brought up to speed by Eight.

'The best plan,' said another Five.

'We've been looking forward to this show!' said another.

Eight thrust its arm out and pointed down the tunnel to an area where Eight deemed the Tekktate to be slightly less dense. Five slinked off and began to drill the alcove big enough to fit the group in safely. It was slower work than previously, as the Tekktate was still a little denser than before but Five ploughed on and was soon done.

'When you are ready, Lewis,' Eight said.

Lewis walked across to the machine and laid his hands on its outer casing. He found that, if he relaxed, he could control the flow of Kora more easily and it required less effort. However, Lewis had never been very good at relaxing and the green charge erupted from his hands in highly intense but spluttery bursts.

Eight felt the power soaring through it once more and nodded to Lewis when it thought it had enough. Lewis tried to withdraw his hands but found that they would not move and the green continued to burst forth; his hands seemed to be magnetised to the machine. Eight tried to wriggle its body free and Lewis tried to wriggle his hands free, but to no avail - until suddenly they both came loose with a large popping noise.

'Sorry,' Lewis said, with some embarrassment.

'Think nothing of it,' replied Eight, its three dials now brightly sparking with green energy - which made it look somewhat demented. It strode off down the tunnel whilst the children and Five stole into the alcove that Five had drilled at a 45 degree-angle to provide maximum protection.

Eight stood still in what it deemed to be precisely the correct spot for the bomb to have most effect. Once it had gathered a healthy dose of Tekktate from the ground, the noises within it started slowly; the rumbling, the pounding, the screeching of grinding and mixing. The noises changed and built in intensity - it now sounded as though multiple objects were rattling around, but the chaotic rattling soon turned to a rhythmic rolling and became faster and faster and faster until these objects all collided with bang after bang and were joined together. The rolling sounds gave way to just one large sound, which seemed slower because of its increased size but was actually even faster and getting faster still. The sounds of sloshing and some more banging and rattling joined in and, even though they were some distance down the tunnel, the children covered their ears as the ramshackle orchestra once again played its discordant tune.

The noises stopped suddenly, and there was a pause. Then the hiss of a flap and a great thud as a very, very large round and black sphere landed on the ground at Eight's feet. The children clenched tightly, but kept their eyes open, desperate to see the effects of the bomb.

Eight looked down at its creation and its dials widened as it realised what it had done, and simply uttered:

'Uh-oh!'

Before Eight could even take a step, the bomb exploded in an enormous bright green flash, and the hulk of Eight's blackened shell flew past the alcove at an incredible speed and kept going all the way back along the tunnel.

Kat, panicking, rushed towards Eight, with Artie and Five in hot pursuit. Lewis, still feeling a little weak, finally brought up the rear.

Kat bent down over the machine, which seemed to be out cold, although more strange noises were coming from within. The noises grew louder - Eight's dials lit up, and Kat soon realised that the machine was, in fact, laughing. Its laughing grew louder, and it sat up to look at the children.

'Incredible,' it said, still chuckling. 'Ah. I had forgotten just how much fun it was to travel by explosion. And that was some journey!'

'I'm sorry,' said Lewis, finally joining the group. 'I may have overdone it.'

Eight ungainly, and with some assistance from Kat and Artie, got back to its hissing feet.

'That is quite alright, Lewis,' it said. 'Now, let us see what progress we may have made.'

As they walked back along the tunnel, with quite the collective spring in their steps, Lewis suddenly had a horrible sinking feeling. For some reason, he expected to be met with the solid end of the tunnel and to be told that the bomb had no effect. Their journey had encountered so many surprises, obstacles and diversions he found it hard to imagine that this would work just as they intended. As such, he was not prepared for the sight that greeted them.

The end of the tunnel had not just been blasted through, it had been obliterated entirely and in front of them was an enormous crater. At the far side of the crater, great pillars rose up into the roof of the cavern, and in the distance, they could see what appeared to be a long and winding, somewhat steep staircase, leading up into the darkness. The far edge of the cavern seemed to drop away sharply, but the pillars followed it all the way down - but to where, they were not close enough to see.

'Ah,' said Eight, pondering and rotating its head back and forth to survey the huge crater. 'It would appear that the density of the Kora transferred from Lewis, was rather more extreme than I had calculated for.'

Artie stared at the huge vista in front of him, delighted at the now obstacle-free path. 'What are we looking at here?' he asked, pointing to the large cluster of pillars in the distance.

'These… are the deep foundations of the great city,' Eight explained. 'I do believe we have actually made it.'

Kat sighed with immense relief, but as she did so something moving caught her eye. She looked down at Eight's outer case, just above its now very visible knee-joint to see red sparking around the edges - and a very large dent with an even larger crack running around and through it.

'You've been damaged!' she yelled to Eight. 'But… that's not supposed to be possible. Was the blast too much?'

Eight, unable to see the damage on its lower rear section, tried to rotate and bend in ways it was not designed for. Artie thought it looked a bit like a dog trying to catch its tail.

'I do not believe it was a result of the blast,' said Eight gloomily. 'The blockage, the resistance I have been intermittently feeling - whatever it is - I believe this is more likely the result of continual exposure to the red Kora. The green power does not appear sufficient to repair or unblock it.'

Artie bent down and looked closer at the damage, which was still sparking intensely with redness. 'But... but that means you are not indestructible anymore. Was this Zero's plan all along? To create a new form of power that made the indestructible machines destructible?'

'So that Zero could conquer - and enslave them all...' said Lewis.

CHAPTER ELEVEN
Thirty-Three

Kat looked down the immense staircase. They were now more than half way up it - at least, halfway up the stairs they could actually see in the dim red-soaked half-light. Below her, the stairs disappeared into a deep chasm; it was much too dark to see any firm details - but she was sure that there were interesting structures far below, jutting in all directions. She could not *see* them, but she could *feel* them - residual effects of her connection to this world via the green pool of power.

'What's down there?' she called down loudly, directing the question towards Eight.

'I am unaware of anything of interest that far below the city,' responded Eight. The machine turned its head to look down, rotated its three dials and zoomed its lens in and out in an attempt to focus on whatever the girl thought was deep below them. Eight's answer did not sit comfortably with Kat - the machine either did not know or was not willing to divulge more secrets about this ancient world. She could feel something was down there. She just knew it.

Lewis and Eight brought up the rear of the group, both ascending the staircase at their own, slow pace. Kat looked across the large crater they had crossed; Lewis had struggled again for energy and so they had virtually emptied the second knapsack of food to ensure they all had enough energy for the daunting ascent. Eight was still sparking with red, but to the machine's credit, it never grumbled despite how much more difficult the journey must have been with only one fully working leg. Kat looked at the thin film of red charge coursing over the surface of the stairs, and the rage built up in her. All she could imagine was Zero, in its tower surrounded by and protected by an army of corrupted comrades, looking down at the world it had broken through its new, deadly power creation. How were they using this power, right now? What chaos were they causing in the city above?

She tried to push the image aside and looked up the staircase to judge how much further they still had to go. Five was at the head of the group, coiling and springing up several chunky steps at once, then stopping, turning and waiting for the rest to catch up - like an eager and faithful dog would do running up a hill with its owners. If it had a tail it would wag it, Kat thought.

Kat noticed that Artie, just ahead of her, was surprisingly quiet - he had been ever since they had understood Zero's true motives and the devastating power of the red Kora. In fact, no-one had said very much since then; they were all absorbing the new reality that this world - a world without any form of death or destruction - was perhaps gone forever, replaced by something far more dangerous and unsettling. There must be a way to fix this, she thought - their mission now was not just to unjam the world and find a way home, but somehow to rid it of all the red Kora too. It may be the only way to save the machines from ultimate destruction.

'Here!' shouted Five down from above. 'We think this is it!'

'It could be!' yelled another Five.

'No doubt about it!' said another.

The group quickened their pace and soon caught up with the tall machine, who had reached the top stair and then sprung along the short tunnel. It had stuck its pointed head into a space in the tunnel roof and ratcheted up so that it could see further. It then began another conversation with itself.

'We can see a little street, and some buildings, and... it is all very empty.'

'Now might be a good time to go up.'

'While there is nothing around.'

'No Zero.'

'None of Zero's awful friends.'

Artie, losing patience, gently shoved Five over a little and started to climb up the tall machine - using the coils of its body like the rungs of a ladder - so that he could see for himself.

'Hey!' said Five, indignantly.

'Rude...' said another.

Artie popped his head up through the gap and saw that he was looking out of some sort of service opening. In his world, these would be covers that led to drains to let excess water seep away, but in this world the exact purpose of it escaped him. The brightness of the day hurt his eyes and took quite some time to adjust to. He squinted around and confirmed everything that the Fives had reported.

'It's safe,' he whispered before disappearing up through the opening. 'Come on.'

Kat followed his lead, and started to climb up Five, apologising as she went. Lewis came after, more slowly, and then Five sprung itself up through the hole, flipped over, bent down, uncoiled itself even further and reached in to haul Eight up onto street level by recoiling and recompressing itself tightly.

Kat, her eyes smarting with the light, saw that it was not really a street at all, but more like an alleyway. It was deserted. Everything was completely still and silent; thin red washed over every dark, highly polished surface just as it had in the wilderness, and underground.

'What's the plan?' Kat whispered, more to Eight than anyone else in the group. Now that they were here, exposed in the lion's den, she felt a strong desire to become completely invisible.

'I believe that we should move directly to the control tower via the shortest route possible, keeping entirely out of sight and away from wide open spaces,' it said, before realising its plan had already been blown to pieces. Artie had walked away from the group and stood beyond the end of the alleyway, in the middle of the adjoining street and was looking up and all around him, his mouth hanging wide open.

Eight slapped its hand to the top of its head casing, looked at its appendage questioningly and then found itself gazing at Kat. The machine was initially unsure how it even knew what this gesture meant, but then realised it was another part of the children that now lived inside its programming.

Kat had slinked alongside the buildings of the alleyway towards where Artie stood. She was just about to call out to him, perhaps even to scold him, as quietly as she could, when she saw what he saw.

Whilst the alleyway was deserted, the main street was anything but. Machines of all shapes and sizes littered the main thoroughfare. The sides of many buildings were clad in various machines, seemingly going about their everyday functions, but completely frozen in place. The street and every building were all so clean and so polished it made the whole place look quite unreal. If Time had been active, everything would gleam in the light so brightly her eyes would not be able to cope. As it was, with Time stuck, the light lit everything - but nothing gleamed, reflected or refracted quite as it should. Her brain thought it was impossible but was soon distracted by the multitude of other impossible sights amongst the winding streets and layers and layers of buildings and structures that seemed to go on for miles and stretched so high up that she could not see all their tops.

Every building she could see nearby was entirely different from the one beside or opposite. In front of her was a building shaped like a series of shark's fins all lined up in a row and growing increasing tall as they went, but across from that strange arrangement was a building made of hexagonal and octagonal pods - all stacked on top of one another like some kind of abstracted honeycomb. Next to that was a very tall building shaped like the letter U, but asymmetrical and resting perfectly on a single small sphere. She turned to look behind her and saw an even taller building that seemed to twist around itself more times than her eyes could account for. The building that adjoined that one was flat and unremarkable except that it was full of concave sphere-shapes, seemingly randomly dotted all over its surface like swiss cheese. Inside those concave spaces all manner of platforms and balconies and ramps jutted out and connected to each other. As she widened her gaze she saw that the majority of buildings were bizarrely gravity-defying; many were madly top heavy or spiralised and cantilevered so extremely they should have simply fallen down. She wondered that should Time restart, would any of them truly fall - but she knew that this was all a result of extraordinarily precise machine engineering. She found it hard to continue to look at such a brain-melting vista and so she cast her gaze elsewhere.

Down near her feet, was the smallest machine she had seen so far, as small as a little bird but very unbirdlike in form. She bent down to examine it and saw that it appeared to be in the middle of polishing the surface of the street - with one tiny appendage that was shaped and bristled like a brush - with the finest strands of Tekktate imaginable.

'Well, you've done an incredible job for one so small,' she whispered to it, looking at the tiny machine within this vast, spotlessly clean city. It was just then she realised that keeping the city clean was obviously of great importance to the race of machines. Stuck to the side of a building to her left, almost half-way up, was an enormous tentacle-shaped machine, storeys and storeys tall. It was just hanging there, its top-half attached to the building by what looked to be mechanised suckers, and it was twisted around the middle so that the suckers on the bottom half were facing out from the building. On the flipside of its bottom half were more bristled strands of Tekktate, huge, and it also appeared to be stuck in the midst of polishing - floors and floors of the building all at the same time.

'Ah...' she whispered, bending down to the little machine again. 'You had some help.'

Something in the sky above caught her eye, and she wondered how she had initially missed the great dark patch it cast on the street below. It hung in mid-air and, from below, appeared to be ribbed like a blimp. But it was very much the wrong shape to be a blimp; it was much wider, somewhat flatter and uneven - although it was hard to make out its exact shape from below due to its sheer size - it was almost as long as some of the buildings were tall. It had strange things sticking out either side and another larger thing sticking out of what was probably its back-end. She felt that she almost knew the shape, and she racked her brain for what it reminded her of; an image came to her that was not quite correct but was as close as she could manage. It was a whale - mechanical and much, much bigger - flying through the air just as the creature might swim through the ocean in her own world. In its wake, slipstreaming, were a host of black dots - what she presumed were other, much smaller flying, hovering or gliding machines - but they were far too small to make out from so far below. Kat was so transfixed by the bizarre sight that she did not notice Eight was now standing beside her.

'Ah yes,' it said. 'The 10:43 from Grand Central. Impossible to tell if it was running on time or not. It always is, however, and to the millisecond.'

'It's a bus?' asked Kat, still staring upwards, gobsmacked.

Eight whirred and clunked, searching its database once more. 'Transport in a communal vehicle,' it relayed from its internal dictionary. 'Yes, it is a bus. Filled with many other machines, most likely.'

Kat looked around once again. On the far side of the street, propped up against the side of another building, was a long, very thin machine with odd protrusions sticking out in very regular intervals. On, or just above, many of these protrusions was an assortment of many other small machines, all in a line - as regular as you like. The machine that was highest up was mid-stride, having seemingly leapt from the top protrusion onto a ledge on the side of the building. The line of little machines appeared to be using the long, larger machine as a ladder to reach the upper levels of the building, similarly to how the children had used Five to reach street level.

Kat's head was spinning with the array of little and large machines that met her eyes, and with every size in-between. She turned again and looked even higher up; balanced delicately between two buildings, covering the full width of the street, was a machine that initially looked to her like some sort of spider - it certainly had appendages that were very spidery, but Kat counted many more than eight; 10, 12... no, 16 at least. She was sure there were even more on the far side of its body that she could not fully see. The body of this machine was, however, nothing like any spider she had ever seen. It was far more segmented, long, snaked through its many legs and curled downwards to face the street. From what may have been its head, ('how on earth can you tell the front from the back on most of these machines?' she asked herself), were multiple strands of the finest Tekktate, and they appeared to be forming a walkway that was only half-constructed - strung between the two buildings.

'A spiderpillar machine that spins new parts of buildings just like a spider spins a web,' she said out loud. 'Well, that makes just as much sense as anything else here.'

Eight moved even closer to her side and lowered its voice. 'We are too exposed here and we have lingered too long; I fear we are... what is the phrase?'

'Pushing our luck?' said Lewis, who had finally broken cover from the empty alleyway to join the group and revel in the fascinating, inexplicable sights all around.

Eight nodded. 'Pushing our luck. Come. Let us go.'

Before the words of warning had even escaped his mouth, Lewis' legs trembled like jelly as the world shook noisily in the throes of yet another Timequake. It was brief and not as severe as the last one - just a few seconds, but in those few seconds, everything shifted.

The whalebus arced, dived and swept around the spire of a building, with a flurry of little winged machines darting after it. The spiderpillar spun another balustrade of the walkway, and at least three little machines jumped up onto the ledge from the ladder-like machine propped against the building. Everything suddenly froze once again, but not before Artie was knocked completely off his feet high into the air by a round but small wheel-like machine that had weaved its way at immense speed through the crowd of machines littered across the street.

'Trakka-blart!' it yelled as it careered into Artie and sent him flying before stopping dead.

Kat rushed over to Artie and helped him back to his feet.

'Are you ok?' she asked.

Artie groaned and winced in pain but nodded to signal that he was fine.

'Interesting...' mused Eight, studying the again frozen wheel-like machine.

'What did it say?' asked Artie, rubbing his smarting behind and then his stiff neck.

'The closest translation is "coming through",' said Eight. 'Did you notice that, in those few seconds when Time resumed, the machines all carried on exactly as they had been before Time froze. No pause, no awakening, no understanding that anything was wrong at all.'

'What could that mean?' asked a Five.

'Ooh, we think we know,' said another Five, uncoiling its arm and stretching its hand to the sky.

'What are you doing?' asked a different Five.

Five looked up at its outstretched hand.

'We have no idea,' Five said, realising that the gesture it was performing made no sense to it.

Kat giggled, knowing exactly what the machine was doing - and that she was, of course, partly responsible.

Eight shook its head, its servos grinding, and spoke first to deny Five its moment of glory. 'I believe that the reason these machines do not seem to have noticed the world has frozen - is our proximity to the control tower - the centre of the initial corruption. Far away, in the wilderness, the effects of Time jamming took, well, *time* to take hold; it slowed as it spread. But here, so close to the epicentre, the effect was immediate. These poor machines have no idea that the world has been broken at all.'

Five sulked. 'We were going to say exactly that, we were...'

'Poor machines?' asked Lewis, interrupting. 'Maybe they're the lucky ones. They have no knowledge of Zero. No fear of it. To them, the world is still perfect.'

'How can we be sure?' asked Artie. 'No offence, Eight - but what you've said is just another guess.'

'Maybe we should awaken one of them?' said Kat, looking around. 'Which one?'

'That... is a dangerous course of action,' advised Eight, sternly. 'We have no means to determine which, if any, of these machines are still trustworthy. And which may have been corrupted by Zero.'

'Well, if they had been corrupted, surely they wouldn't be frozen...' said Artie, rather cockily.

Eight studied the boy before responding. 'Your logic has merit Artie,' it said. 'But it too is based on assumption rather than hard evidence.'

'We think it is worth the risk,' said Five.

'You would,' said another Five.

'Enough!' said Kat impatiently, still feeling far too exposed. 'We take a vote. All in favour of awakening one of the machines so we can ask them what they know?' She shot her hand up into the air, and Artie's soon followed hers.

Lewis' hand stayed firmly down by his side, but in truth he was not sure what the right thing to do was. The thought of accidentally awakening one of Zero's spies made him shiver.

'How many votes do we get?' asked Five.

'Just one!' said Kat forcefully.

'Oh, ok,' said the tall machine, uncoiling multiple arms and shooting them all towards the sky anyway.

'Motion carried,' said Artie. 'Now, which one do we awaken?'

'This one is closest,' said Kat, pointing to the wheeled machine that had sent Artie flying. She approached it and looked more closely, noticing that whilst it was clearly a slick and sleek wheel of some sort, it differed from those of her bicycle or those of the family car. For one thing it was not a complete circle - it was shaped somewhere in-between the letter O and the letter C, and it did not have spokes that spun out from the centre. Instead the central structures spun from one side of the wheel to the other and were in a sort of wave formation. Around its rim were three visually different forms of Tekktate and there were slight gaps in-between each type. The central section was incredibly smooth and polished, but both outer sections had regular criss-crossed patterns everywhere on their blackened surfaces. She could not see any dials or protrusions that may act as eyes or limbs anywhere, but she did notice some sparse markings running vertically down the central section.

'It has symbols on it, but some appear to be missing,' she said. 'There are gaps that look like there should be something there.'

Eight studied the symbols on the machine's body. 'You are correct, Kat. There are marks where there should be symbols - here, here and here, but they are oddly missing. I can only see a Tronk, a Snart, another Tronk and then a Sqwart. Sorry, I mean three dash three L'.

Artie rubbed his sore behind and neck again. 'Ok - let's awaken the round three-three thing then. I can tell it off for being so careless.'

Lewis suddenly felt eight eyes and dials all look at him expectantly, but he also felt as though every machine around, frozen or not, was also staring directly at him, waiting. He approached the wheel-machine cautiously, knowing what he must do. It was one thing to know that being relaxed helped him control the flow of positive power, but another thing entirely to actually be able to do it.

'Just a tiny burst,' cautioned Kat. 'We don't want it to have too much in case we can't trust it.'

Lewis nodded in understanding and gently laid his hands on the machine. A tiny burst of positive power slipped gently from his hands in an entirely controlled manner. Lewis felt himself smile, knowing that he had done it perfectly this time.

The wheel machine instantly powered up and sped off out of sight, leaving the group reeling from their own stupidity.

'Oh,' said Eight sheepishly and once more slapping its hand to its head. 'We did not fully consider that possibility.'

Artie was just about to say something he probably should not, but instead started to point. 'Look!'

The wheel-machine was trundling back into sight, wheeling its way around the scattered frozen machines of the street, studying them all and looking thoroughly confused. As it rounded a rather large machine a few metres away, it saw the group, unfrozen - and spoke from a thin, vertical slot running down the centre of its body.

'YouWhoThen?' it said, so very quickly the group did not initially understand. An area just above the vertical slot that behaved like a mouth lit up in a shifting, ever-changing array of dots of lights as it spoke.

'Good day to you,' said Eight as politely as it could. 'If you would be so kind, we are in need of your assistance.'

'YouSpeakNotFabrakkan?' said the machine, even more confused but just as quickly. 'HowMeYouUnderstand?'

'You are not speaking Fabrakkan either, my friend,' Eight continued. 'You have, via the power of touch, learned some of a new language.'

'WellThatSomething!' responded the wheel, sounding rather pleased at this incredible thing. 'WhatYouNeed?'

'Please, slow down,' urged Kat, struggling to keep up with the wheel's abrupt topsy-turvy words. Kat and Lewis now realised that the transference of their knowledge to the machines was entirely down to something inside the green Kora.

'Slow?' replied the wheel. 'SlowNotMeUsual.' The machine's lights altered shape again and it seemed to be concentrating hard. 'Is better this?' it asked.

Kat nodded then asked. 'Yes, a little, thanks. What's your name?'

The machine tried to talk as slowly as it could, but the speed of its voice came out all over the place. 'MyDesignationIs, in language I KnowNow, WH3-3L5. And I WillHelp if can I.'

'Why is some of your designation missing from your chassis?' asked Artie. 'Surely they haven't broken off?'

'NeverPutOn,' said the machine. 'No time to wait. DidNotNeed. Places to be. ThingsToDeliver!'

'Ah,' said Eight. 'You are a distribution machine. That explains a lot. Built for speed.'

'Yes,' it replied. 'MissedNever a DeliverySlot.'

Kat felt that growing feeling again where she wanted more than anything to become invisible and urged the now larger group to return to the empty alleyway, which they did. When she felt that they were safely out of sight of clusters of machines that could be masking Zero's spies, she relayed to the new machine everything they knew about the frozen world, Zero and their plans to unjam it. Without even realising she was doing it, she had slipped into the habit of calling the new machine by the nickname she felt was right for it - Thirty-Three.

'Thirty-Three...' it mused, finally sliding into a more consistent speed of talking, and tripping over its words a little less. 'No-one called me anything nice ever. Just called me messenger - very impersonal. Hmmm, Thirty-Three. It I like!'

'So will you help us?' asked Kat. 'What do you know?'

As it turned out, Thirty-Three knew very little of use at all. Eight's assumption that the Time-freeze was instantaneous the closer to the control tower it happened was indeed correct and seemed to be confirmed by the wheeled machine's lack of knowledge.

'You know,' Thirty-Three said whilst rotating to face each of the children in turn. 'Fleshbots - you are familiar. I sure I meet like you before. Long, long time ago.'

The children all looked at one another, before addressing Thirty-Three.

'A man?' asked Lewis.

'A tall, thin man?' asked Kat.

'With long, white hair?' asked Artie.

'Let me see,' thought Thirty-Three as it made a whole host of noises similar to Eight did when searching its database. The whirring and clicking were sharply interrupted by a horrible grinding noise that signalled something was wrong.

'Strange,' said Thirty-Three. 'Not access those files for reason odd.'

It tried again, but after a few seconds the same horrid grinding noise erupted, disappointing the assembled group.

Thirty-Three continued. 'Sure I know *where* saw fleshbot, though. Can take you there. As machine of delivery I see all this city many times. Not a street not crossed, not a building not entered, not a floor not delivered to. Every shortcut, every access - recorded inside me.'

'What should we do?' asked Five.

'To the fleshbot or the control tower?' said another Five.

'Please stop calling us fleshbots,' said Kat. 'It's a horrible word. And we're not 'bots. We're humans.'

'The control tower,' Eight said authoritatively. 'I am sorry children but restoring Time must still be the priority. We shall search for the professor and a means to return you home once Fabrakka is made safe again.'

Kat nodded, knowing that Eight was of course correct. Artie nodded too, and finally Lewis added his own nods that signalled the end of this round of silent voting.

'Now,' said Eight. 'Thirty-Three. Is there a secondary entrance to the control tower? Some way in without being seen by Zero or its spies.'

Thirty-Three rolled back and forward on the spot with excitement, revving.

'MostCertainlyIs!'

CHAPTER TWELVE

The Control Tower

Lewis turned, and then turned again, sure that he saw something moving out of the corner of his eye. But nothing had moved - everything was just as frozen as it had been two seconds ago.

'This way,' Thirty-Three urged as it wheeled its way around the corner of the building towards the rear entrance. There were far fewer machines around this part of the city; the control tower was very central and by far the tallest, spindliest and most mind-bendingly twisted building of all the gravity-defying structures, but the area surrounding it was not nearly as full of assorted contraptions or developments as the main thoroughfare that led to it.

'Quietly,' said Kat, looking intently at Five and Thirty-Three in particular. She only realised after the words had left her mouth what an odd thing it was to say. In the vacuum of no-Time, there was no real noise that carried - the sounds the group made could not travel far beyond the thin bubble of Time that the green allowed to radiate from them; but in this city occupied or infiltrated by potential spies, the consequences of unwanted noise seemed a very different prospect than out in the uninhabited wilderness.

'Here,' Thirty-Three said, and prised open the modestly sized door to allow the group in - the door was a shape Kat had certainly never seen before. Five had to bend over almost double and coil itself as tightly as possible to be able to fit through the oddly-shaped opening.

As they filed in, one-by-one, with Thirty-Three propping open the door, Lewis suddenly feared that this approach could be a grave mistake. The hairs on the back of his neck prickled and he looked around frantically once more, convinced he could feel movement even if he could not see it. He held the door, and ushered Thirty-Three in ahead of him, not wanting to be closely followed by a machine he did not yet have reason to fully trust.

'What now?' asked Artie.

'Elevator along here, at side of atrium far. Only delivery or service machines use, so us will keep hidden - allow to reach upper floors more quick,' replied Thirty-Three. The machine was now doing a little better in terms of its speaking speed with this newly acquired language, but still had not quite grasped the correct order of things.

Thirty-Three gestured for them all to follow, and it rolled along the triangular corridor towards the main atrium. They passed a few isolated frozen machines on the way, but the number of machines overall seemed to be thinning out, and the group chose to avoid them and prioritise reaching the control room.

If anything, the more scattered machines made Lewis even more nervous. None of them looked threatening in any way, but Lewis had learned long ago not to judge anyone, (or anything) by their seemingly innocent looks. The machines they had encountered so far were generally very good natured, but also quite startling in ways he would not have expected. Eight did not have a sharp edge anywhere on its outer casing, yet its speciality was making destructive bombs that could rip the ground apart. Conversely, Five had the sharpest point at the tip of its head that Lewis had ever seen, (and had no desire to touch) yet it spent much of its time talking - or arguing - with itself rather than pointing its weaponised head in a threatening manner. Thirty-Three? Well, it was too soon to tell. And Zero? Lewis shivered at the thought of the mysterious machine again, whose motives for breaking and conquering this peaceful world were unfathomable to him.

Lewis took a deep breath. He felt so ill-prepared for the path the group was now on, that he wanted to stop, regroup, form a completely new plan and put off this reckless sortie for another day. His heart sank when Thirty-Three indicated that they had reached the service elevator that would deliver them up the tower and reach the control room in a matter of minutes, once repowered.

'Lewis…' Kat began, '…we need your power to start the elevator.'

Lewis stepped forward and placed his hands on the panel on the wall near the doors and let the positive power flow. He was more on edge than the last time and the green charge stuttered out of him in an uncontrolled manner that meant he was not really sure how much he had released. It certainly did not feel like as much came out as he had wanted. The elevator doors slid open, and the group filed into a small and cramped dark space. As the doors slid back together, Lewis gulped.

'Oh, hello,' said a pleasant voice seemingly from nowhere. 'What an odd bunch you are! Now, where to today?'

Lewis looked around for the disembodied voice, and slowly realised that it was the elevator talking. It had not occurred to him that elevators would talk, but it was, of course, a machine just like any other on Fabrakka.

'To the top, please,' said Kat politely.

'Ok,' replied the elevator. 'But I only go so far; top floors only via the dedicated elevator. Hmmm... you look a strange creature, but your grasp of Fabrakkan is good.'

Eight explained, as succinctly as it could, the language and transference power of green Kora to the elevator, and then quickly indicated that they were all ready to go up.

The elevator shot up at an incredible speed, so fast that the children could not keep their balance and had to cling on to the walls.

'Slower!' yelled Artie to the elevator. 'Much, much slower!'

The elevator slowed so suddenly that their feet actually left the floor for a second.

'Oh, sorry,' said the elevator. 'Not sure where such a rush of energy came from. Better?'

The elevator glided gently upwards and the group sighed collective relief.

'Much,' said Artie. 'Thanks.'

Light suddenly flooded into the elevator as it glided past a floor and they realised that one side of the elevator was entirely transparent - made of a form of pale Tekktate that was very glassy but with a slightly darkened tint. Fabrakka lay beneath them, spread out in all its vast glory. Kat could see the whalebus, this time a little from above, and saw that the black dots in its wake were an assortment of machines that, whilst they were all completely unique, were also bizarre mashups of part-bird-like, part-flying-insect-like and often part-helicopter-like machines.

The transparent side of the elevator opened up onto the Fabrakka they had not crossed. The cityscape occupied most of their view - it stretched for miles and miles and was a confusing mass of uniquely shaped constructions, but just at the fringes they could see more red-washed wilderness, and then looming beyond it were massive mountainous areas with very aggressive looking ridges and jagged, needle-like stacks. Some of the stacks poked through the clouds, and Kat pressed herself against the glassy surface to see better. She squinted and peered and could swear she saw even more structures hanging *inside* the distant clouds.

'That is the city of Kasperitakk,' Eight said. 'It is where many, ahem, *machines of age* choose to dwell to consider and shape their futures, and in many cases - become Makers. Machines that leave Kasperitakk are often quite different in form and evolved in function than when they first arrived there.'

Kat considered Eight's words, and the group were silent for a short time as they looked out on the resplendent wonder of the motionless world. Kat realised Fabrakka was even vaster, denser, more layered and more inexplicable than she could have ever imagined.

'Like some music?' asked the elevator, breaking the contemplative silence. Before any of the group could reply it had begun to emit noises that seemed to the children to be a random thrashing of banging, pounding and grinding.

'Oh, we like this one,' said Five, and it began tapping its large foot, uncoiling parts of itself and swaying around, and Thirty-Three rolled a little back and forward in time to the raucous banging. Artie was just beginning to decipher what may have been a melody in there somewhere, when Kat replied.

'No thanks!' she said, loudly and the music ceased.

'Suit yourself,' said the elevator.

The elevator ride took much longer than Lewis expected, and he felt some brief relief that whatever danger lay in the main control room was still at arm's length. They passed the first layer of static cloud cover and Fabrakka beneath vanished from sight.

After a few more minutes, where nothing was said and little could be seen, Artie moved closer to Kat and whispered to her. 'Is it just me, or is this elevator getting slower?'

Kat sensed that he was right. The elevator had been gradually slowing and, although she knew that the journey up the immense tower would take some time, they should surely have been there by now.

'Erm, how much longer?' asked Kat to the elevator.

'Oh, still a few floors,' it replied. 'Would you like to go a little faster?'

'Yes, please,' said Kat.

'No, thanks,' thought Lewis.

Kat did not feel any change in speed initially, but then, after a few moments, she did. The elevator was getting slower still - and soon she felt as though they were not moving at all.

'Is there a problem?' she asked the elevator. It did not reply.

'We can take that as a yes, then,' said Artie. 'I think we've stopped dead. Lewis, more power please.'

Lewis, reluctantly, laid his hands on the wall and released the power. Nothing came. He tried to relax, closed his eyes and just let it flow. Nothing. He looked at his hands, unsure if it was his unease preventing him from letting the Kora out, or if he had actually run dry.

'Come on, Lewis,' urged Artie. 'What's the hold up?'

'I… I think… I'm out,' he replied.

'Oh,' said Kat, knowing only too well what that felt like. To have such wonderful power running through you, being part of you - and then to have it leave, making you feel so empty inside was just like having your best friend suddenly move away to another school in another town.

'Let's all try together,' she suggested, hoping not only that it would work, but that it would make Lewis feel better. Artie knew he had no green charge left inside him but joined in anyway and all three children together tried to let the power flow from them into the elevator. Nothing happened.

'We're stuck,' said Lewis in a bouncy voice that actually made him sound happy at the thought.

'Maybe we can prise the door open?' Artie asked. 'What do we have that's very sharp and thin and could maybe slip into this thin crack of the door?'

All eyes and dials turned to Five and its razor-sharp, precise drill-bit head. Five however, (all of them), seemed entirely unaware of the group's meaning and said nothing. It still seemed to be swaying and humming along to the elevator music that had long since stopped.

'Five!' yelled Kat, losing patience once more.

'Oh, right,' a Five finally said.

'We understand!' said another.

'Erm... what are we doing?' asked another.

Artie thrust his hand forward pointing his finger at Five, then moved it rapidly across the elevator and pointed directly at the thin join between the door sections.

'Oh, right,' Five said again and moved towards the door. There was not a lot of space in the modest sized service elevator and so the entire group had to move around to let the tall machine pass by.

'Pardon me,' said Five.

'Sorry.'

'Watch your feet.'

'Argh, my toe!'

'Sorry.'

'Just on your left, here.'

'Thanks.'

Five eyed the thin slip where the doors joined, seemingly deep in thought.

'Nothing else for it,' it said and bent over - plunging the tip of its head into the gap and began drilling at great speed.

The grinding noise was unbearable and although the children covered their ears, it still hurt their heads. Soon though, the thin gap became a wide gap and Eight and the children grabbed each side of the door and wrenched it fully open.

Panting, gasping and hissing - they looked at the struts of the solid floor that now faced them. The elevator had stopped between two floors - the gap above them was larger, but they would have to climb up to it. The gap below was thinner and harder to fit through, but much easier to reach.

'Down,' said Lewis.

'Up,' said Artie.

'The children and Five should have little problem reaching the upper floor,' said Eight. 'However, that proves a little tougher for our wheeled friend here and I.'

'I can haul you up, no problem,' said Five.

'Indeed,' said Eight. 'However, this may be an ideal opportunity for us to reconnoitre over more ground and see… how do you say… the lay of the land?'

'What?' said Lewis.

'It thinks we should split up and look around before deciding how best to approach the control room,' said Artie.

'Precisely,' said Eight.

Lewis did not like the idea of the group being separated at all, but he did not feel prepared to launch an assault of any kind on a control room filled with malevolent corrupted machines, and so fully backed this plan.

'Yes,' he said, unusually assertively. 'We need to know exactly what we are facing before we, well, face it.'

The group all nodded - except Thirty-Three who rolled back and forth, which Kat realised was its physical way of showing that it agreed.

Eight, very ungainly - and hissing from many of its invisible seams - clambered down through the smaller opening onto the lower floor. Thirty-Three revved hard, then burst forward, leaned onto its side and slid screeching through the gap then landed and skidded to a halt with a flourish.

'Subtle,' said Artie, rolling his eyes.

Five uncoiled multiple arms and helped lift the three children up through the gap all at the same time whilst also pulling itself up.

'Now,' said Eight quietly. 'Keep out of sight. Look around. Take note of how many machines there are, and what they are. Try to find any unobvious ways to the main control room. And look for ways to escape the tower, should things not appear to be in our favour. We clearly cannot use this method of travel again.'

'Ok,' said Artie. 'We will meet up again in a safe space just outside of the control room. If there is one...'

Artie, Lewis, Kat and Five moved slowly along the somewhat angular but also rather twisted corridor. Artie took point, although Five, (being so tall) found it hard to move at such a slow speed and, (without even trying to) kept overtaking Artie. Lewis felt too exposed at the rear and wanted to move forward along the line - but that meant Kat would be last, so he stayed back to ensure he could see her at all times. He felt as though something was always right behind him - so close he could feel it - but every time he turned to look there was nothing there.

They reached another set of doors, without incident, and without even seeing any other immobile machines along the way. They realised that these doors were for the dedicated elevator to the control room the service elevator had mentioned.

'What now?' asked Kat.

'Well… we have no power to restart it, so we have to find another way up,' said Artie. 'Look for stairs, or a ramp - maybe something to climb.'

'No power…' said Lewis, panicking a little. 'Exactly how are we going to fight whatever lies in wait in the control room without any power? We're just kids!'

Artie shrugged his shoulders, but then said, 'One step at a time. Let's just focus on getting there and seeing what's what. Then we can make plans when we know more. Look - what's that over there?'

There was an opening at the end of the corridor - not a door as such, more like an archway that dog-legged and seemed to ramp upwards as it snaked out of sight. The group approached the entrance to this new, much more organic-feeling corridor, and slowly crept around the bend.

The corridor was thankfully empty - but as they moved along it, gently rising all the time, they saw that there were many offshoots of other corridors leading away from the main one - some up and some down. They could not see where these offshoots led too, but the whole area had suddenly become a tangled spider-web of routes.

'Perfect place for an ambush,' said Artie, looking all around.

Lewis gulped and frantically spun around trying to see everywhere all at once. 'Let's not come back this way,' he said, and to his surprise Artie agreed with frantic nods of his head.

'Let's push on,' said Kat, nervously looking along the many corridors leading in multiple directions. 'It's weird - I don't like it here.'

It was not long before the vaulted, undulating corridor became much less tangled and soon it ended, opening up into a more regular-shaped flat corridor. They had been elevated another few floors without even realising it and in the distance, they could see large heavy-set doors that looked quite important.

'The control room?' asked Artie, almost to himself.

Lewis hoped not and found that his legs would not move as he instructed them - moving instead slower and slower. He realised that he was becoming detached from the group and he wanted to speed up and be closer to Kat, but his legs would not play ball. Suddenly, from behind he felt a touch - a heavy weight that pressed his shoulder down towards the ground. His heart froze.

'Shhh...' said Eight. 'It is only Thirty-Three and I. What did you see?'

Lewis shook his head frantically. The words would not come, but as the icy shock wore off, he was able to form a few mumbled words.

'Nothing. Deserted. Feels... not... right.'

Eight nodded in understanding. 'We too, encountered no other machines.' It looked ahead towards the large doors. 'I expected, at the very least, guards or scouts or patrols. Perhaps even Zero itself. Something else is at work here; my logic circuits have not yet been able to decipher this particular enigma.'

The group all regathered at the large doors that they were now sure led into the control room. Surprised that they had met no form of resistance so far, confused by the lack of any patrolling enemy machines, and without any new information with which to form a new strategy, Artie took the lead and quietly cracked open one of the heavy doors to peek inside.

CHAPTER THIRTEEN

Zero Sum Game

The machine studied the controls laid out before it. It entered the code, carefully depressed the small button, pulled the lever hard, turned the dial fully and then pressed and released the large button, just as it had been instructed to do.

It immediately knew that something was wrong; its comrades all around froze as a sea of red instantly burst from every surrounding surface. In that single second since it had released the large button, the machine had performed a thousand processes, and they reduced down to just four key concepts that flooded and overloaded its chipset:

<<< Corrupted.

<<< Betrayed.

<<< Violated.

>>> Shutdown.

Then everything went blank.

*

'I think it's ok,' said Artie, turning back from the crack in the door towards the group. 'There's a group of machines... but they all seem to be... stuck too. I think it might actually be safe.'

Artie cautiously opened the door wider and held it to let the group file in. The control room was surprisingly bright and took them by surprise after all the dark spaces, elevators and twisted corridors. Lewis saw why - the room was encircled with a large panoramic window that looked out across all of Fabrakka. Even from this immense height, he could see the throbbing red-washed terrain through the occasional breaks in the static cloud cover below.

They stepped tentatively, or wheeled gently, around the multitude of frozen machines scattered across the large room. As many of them as there were, they were all quite featureless. They had the same sleek, dark, seamless external elegance of their machine-friends, but the children could not discern any legs or wheels from underneath their cylindrical chassis that draped all the way from their heavy-set shoulders to the ground. At least, the children guessed they were shoulder-like as from beneath them sprung various appendages that were largely arm-like. Some had pairs, others had many more - and where Eight had clamps for hands, these had assortments of other similar mechanical devices. To Lewis (who had spent a lot of time watching his father mending various contraptions), these looked like wrenches, coiled chains, shackles, vices - and in one machine's case - some form of important-looking rod or sceptre simply *was* its arm. None of these features were as disturbing as their face-plates though - there was not a single machine in the room that had any visible dials that could be eyes, or slots that could be mouths. Their stark stillness was unsettling, and Lewis felt even more unnerved that he could not understand how the machines would sense him - if they were unfrozen and functioning.

The red Kora was very thin here, washing over every surface and every machine, but completely placid. It was as far from the torrents of angry waves they had faced in the ocean as it was possible to be. Without the green nearby to provoke it, the red power hardly seemed a threat at all.

'Is this it?' asked Lewis, approaching a particularly bulky machine which was overlooking a large array of controls in the middle of the room. Its heavy, brutish, skewer-like appendage hovered just a centimetre above a large button in the centre of what appeared to be the main control desk.

Eight strode over to Lewis and examined the chassis of the machine, then nodded.

'Here,' it said, pointing to an area near the lower rear part of its head casing. 'v0-LT-2.'

Lewis looked at the huge machine. It was everything he had feared; as heavy as Eight and as tall as Five, as deeply black as it was possible to be - it seemed to reject nearly all light - and it was almost completely covered in sharp edges and tapering spikes. Underneath its chassis (Lewis was sure), lay all manner of weaponised tools, ready to deploy and strike the millisecond it awakened. Perhaps its face-plate even fully opened up into an enormous cannon that blasted white-hot fire and it did not even need to use its hundred other hidden strangling, twisting, crushing devices to win the fight. But the terrible machine just continued to sit there, frozen.

'I don't understand,' said Lewis, scratching his head. 'Why is it frozen? Why are they all frozen?'

'More theory, you understand...' continued Eight, '...but it would appear that their plan did not work out as they perhaps expected.'

'Something went wrong?' asked Kat. 'You mean, they never meant to freeze the world at all?'

'It is possible that freezing the world was the plan all along,' mused Eight. 'But that it was not Zero's plan. An assumption merely… but there is a way to be sure…'. The machine's dials rotated so that the compass needle was at the top and the needle was spinning furiously, and sharply changing between clockwise and anti-clockwise movements.

'No!' said Five, aghast.

'You cannot do that!' said another Five.

'What is it doing?' asked another.

'Maybe only way,' said Thirty-Three despondently, who had also understood Eight's intentions.

The children looked at Eight, confused, but then grasped the other machine's horror as Eight used one of its many secret tools to reveal an invisible seam, then unfasten and lift off the casing of Zero's huge frozen head. All manner of twisted wiring, circuitry, bulbs, valves, lights, diodes, cogs and tubes were exposed - and all crammed on top of each other using almost every available millimetre of space. Inside Zero's head was a near-complete history of every technological advance of this world - hundreds and hundreds and hundreds of years of continuous development somehow still co-operating to make this machine possible.

Lewis stared at the exposed workings of his great fear and realised that beneath the sleek seamless exteriors of all of these machines - Eight, Five and Thirty-Three included - lay such incredible, even unsightly, complexity.

With a delicate touch betraying its bulky clamps, Eight reached into Zero's head and searched. With a satisfying click and then a short hiss, Eight lifted out a large chipset and put it aside. It returned to the inside of Zero's head, and with another click and hiss, lifted out something else.

'A secondary chipset,' Eight said, studying it closely. 'Two sets of logic circuits. The second, a separate dominant set of pre-programmed instructions - rather clumsily integrated I have to say. Designed, no doubt, to override its primary functions until its tasks had been completed. Designed to then fail.'

'You mean... that Zero is just some sort of tool? A victim of something else's plan?' asked Lewis.

Eight nodded, its servos grinding.

'This situation is even graver than we thought,' it said, looking around the room at the many frozen machines. 'Whatever did this, has great power over many, many machines and the ability to control them all. To wilfully violate machines in this way - to override the very fabric of their logic and impulses - is unthinkable.'

Lewis looked around the room, his mind racing and panic building in him. 'What about all these other machines? What if there's another Timequake and they all suddenly awaken? What if they see what we've now done to Zero?'

'Without these chipsets,' said Eight, presenting them in its hand to the group, 'Zero is no longer a threat. Your fear of another Timequake is a real one, Lewis - we must act quickly. We must remove the chipsets from all of these machines, lest they awaken and turn their attention to us.'

'No!' said Five once again.

'Outrageous!' said another.

'These poor machines,' said Kat. 'They've been used, horribly. We don't even know which of these machines may have committed any crimes. Not even Zero.'

'It's unethical,' said Lewis.

'Necessary,' said Artie. 'I agree with Eight. We remove the immediate threat and buy ourselves time and space to act. We can always reinsert their chipsets later when we have regained control of the world. Trial them then to find out the truth. Punish the guilty; free those that are innocent.'

'Crimes. Ethics. Trials. Guilty. Innocent. I understand the definitions of these words, but there is no precedent on Fabrakka for any of them,' said Eight, whirring, hissing and clunking louder than it ever had before as its compass needle rotated wildly, searching for *something*. 'This situation is the result of the first crime ever to be committed on this world. We have no structures - no rules or laws to deal with events such as...'

Banging and grunting and clicking noises interrupted, as Artie found a seam then, just as Eight had done, unfastened and ripped open the head casing of the nearest machine. With his bare hands, he rummaged through the wiring and removed the chipset. Artie shook and kissed his fingers to lessen the pain in his fingertips caused by the solid Tekktate on his fragile skin. He had no such precise tools as Eight, and his fingers smarted from the effort.

'We can debate all this later! But the safety of Fabrakka is our immediate concern. Let's temporarily disable these potential threats, then figure out how to fix the world.'

There was much grumbling and protesting within the group, and even within Five itself, but they all reluctantly realised they had little choice. The fear of another Timequake forced them to act first and seek forgiveness later. Before long, a pile of chipsets lay before them and a room filled with machines with exposed wiring springing from their heads a stark reminder of the heinous act they had just committed.

'This feels very wrong,' said Kat, despondently.

Artie took a step towards Kat and put his arm on her shoulder. He was about to speak, when Lewis beat him to it.

'We should explore this room, these controls - to understand how we can fix the world,' suggested Lewis, deliberately changing the subject. 'All of these buttons, levers and dials - where do we even start?'

Eight moved across to Zero's large hand, elevated just above an equally large button.

'We can assume that this is the last action Zero performed, and that the majority of the actions we now need to perform can be found somewhere on this control desk. Let me study it more closely - I believe I may be able to work out the sequence.'

'Fat lot of good it will do without any green power,' said Lewis. 'We're all out, and I didn't see any green anywhere in the city on the way here. Did you?'

'No,' said Kat, sounding dejected and shaking her head. For a few moments, no-one said anything, and the silence grew ever more uncomfortable.

'I will return to the ocean,' said Artie. 'Infuse myself with green just as Lewis did. Deliberately this time. That way we may have enough.'

'You can't!' yelled Kat, aghast at the suggestion and new tears threatening to form in her eyes. 'What if you became trapped like Lewis was? Only for even longer? Forever? We have almost no food remaining - you'd never survive!'

'And it's so far back to travel,' said Lewis. 'I think you'd run out of food before you even got to the ocean.'

'Then what would you suggest?' asked Artie, sulking a little. Neither Kat nor Lewis could offer a new suggestion and so Artie walked across to the large window by himself and looked over Fabrakka, stuck for an obvious way forward.

'Sorry interrupt,' said Thirty-Three softly, as it wheeled towards Kat and Lewis. 'But remind you fleshbo... mean, children; saw one your kind long ago at facility near. I take you - maybe in facility is help?'

'Of course!' said Kat, enthused by Thirty-Three's offer. 'It must have been the professor. We are stuck without any green Kora anyway - surely it's worth a look?'

Lewis' stomach rumbled and he felt noticeably weaker. 'It is,' he agreed. 'Eight, have you worked out the sequence yet?'

'Most of it, yes,' said Eight. 'But I believe it will be much easier when at least a little power has been restored to this control desk. Some of the functions are unobvious - it may be necessary to see the functions in operation before truly understanding how they can restore all power to everything.'

Lewis and Kat explained Thirty-Three's offer to Eight and Five, and they collectively agreed that it was the best plan they now had. The only plan in fact, and so they prepared to leave the control room and make their way back down the twisted tower.

'Artie?' Kat called out, realising he was no longer in sight. 'Artie!' she called, panicking.

'I'm here,' he said finally, emerging from a small area near the back of the control room they had not noticed. 'I was just… never mind.'

Artie agreed to the plan, although it seemed to Kat that, oddly, he did not show much enthusiasm or was really paying attention to her. Within just a few moments, the group had left the control room and re-entered, reluctantly, the horrible set of corridors Artie had suggested were perfect for an ambush. Lewis did not feel quite so on edge as before, now that they knew Zero and its followers had been disabled and were possibly not the major threat he had imagined all along. But then, of course, there was another threat out there somewhere - more distant, but also more powerful and clearly far more dangerous. The hairs on the back of his neck began to stand up once more and he found himself looking around nervously as they moved down through the tower. Without any means to repower the elevator, this was going to take quite some time.

*

'I'm starving!' said Lewis. 'Where are we?'

'Very difficult to tell,' replied Eight looking out of the nearest window towards the cloud cover below. 'We may be approximately half-way down the tower. Perhaps a little further on.'

'It doesn't feel like it,' said Lewis. 'Can we stop and have some food?'

'Food, yes,' said Kat. 'Stop, no.' She took the small handful of nuts and an orange that Artie handed her, and he distributed the last of the contents of the knapsack to Lewis and himself.

'That's the last of it,' he said sullenly, and studied the measly collection of nuts in his hand. The thought of running out of real human food and having to default back to the metallic tasting Tekktate discs did not fill him with more energy.

They had been walking for hours, on very little nourishment, following in Thirty-Three's fast wake, always looking for routes downwards - be it ramps or sets of stairs. The wheeled machine took great delight in bumping its way down the stairs at speed or simply, recklessly charging at them as fast as it could. The group felt, overall, lighter and a little happier - as though the anticipation of facing Zero and its band had been pressing them down into the ground; without that immediate pressure there was a sense of relief. Artie, however, had been unusually quiet since the control room - something that was beginning to worry Kat. Perhaps his mind was on this newer, greater threat, or perhaps he was finally thinking of home as she and Lewis had been. She was sure there more to it but decided that particular conversation was best kept for later.

Lewis had felt the relief more than any of them. He had, as usual, worked himself up into a frenzy of worry - making Zero and its comrades bigger, scarier and more threatening than they had perhaps deserved. For the first time in a while, he felt almost happy. The hairs on the back of his neck had slowly returned to normal, and that was also largely down to the fact that they had not encountered a single machine on their journey down the immense tower.

Until now.

They turned a corner and were met by a small group of machines; six of them, all frozen. Again, just like most of the machines in the control room, they appeared largely unremarkable, except for their great bulk; their other talents, whatever they were, lay hidden beneath their dark, cloaked chassis.

The group moved past them, carefully (just in case), but the frozen machines were not their current priority - leaving this tower and making their way to the facility in search of answers and green power was foremost on their minds and circuits. As they reached another set of stairs and began to move down once more, Lewis looked back along the corridor.

'One, two, three, four... five...' he counted. Fear hit him sharply. 'Where is six?' He caught himself. 'Were there six? Did I miscount? Oh, I'm not sure now!' He could feel his neck hairs standing to attention, and the old Lewis returned in full.

The next part of the journey felt much faster to him, possibly spurred on by his desire to get out of this never-ending tower. Every route they took now felt like the perfect place for an ambush. He looked out of the window and saw that the clouds were now high above them, and Fabrakka was visible below them once more. They were making progress, but he still wanted more. His legs quickened in spite of his depleting energy.

Something moved.

Something definitely moved.

A Timequake?

No, there was no rumble, no sound.

Something definitely, definitely moved.

With no further warning, they were surrounded. Three machines had come from nowhere, and like the three points of a triangle, had hemmed the group into a tight pack.

'Quanto skixx takka?' one of the machines barked, in what appeared to the children to be a blunt, highly aggressive tone.

'Kathra tanta zakthra,' replied Eight softly.

'SKATTA! TAKTA!' blurted the largest of the machines and they moved in towards the group in perfect unison. As they moved, the rightmost upper appendage of each of the machines all changed at the same time. The casings reconfigured in an instant - blunt ends became sharp and jagged and Lewis, Kat and Artie stared down the end of their tools, which likely had innocent primary functions, but were now wielded menacingly as terrifying weapons.

'That conversation clearly didn't go well,' thought Artie and immediately stepped in front of both Kat and Lewis.

What happened next seemed a bit of a blur.

With a deafening screech, Thirty-Three sped around one of the aggressors and was behind it before it even noticed the wheeled machine had moved. Five coiled so tightly so quickly and began spinning with such ferocity that the spinning noise was now all that could be heard. Eight did not move, but inside, it had made a series of small bombs in a matter of microseconds that were swirling around its innards. Instead of the bombs colliding into one large bomb as previously, this time Eight expelled them quickly, scattering the small bombs across the floor. The enemy machines twisted and turned around, trying to lunge at and stab Thirty-Three, but the little wheel was too fast, and each machine stabbed thin air. Eight's bombs, whilst small, exploded one by one at the feet of each of the enemies causing small but perfectly placed shockwaves that knocked them all off-balance.

Whilst this was all happening, Kat, Lewis and Artie had hatched their own plan. The three children had moved towards and grabbed the nearby elevator doors and were wresting them apart. It was not as easy as when Five had prised them open with its drill-bit head, but with a strong concerted heave - the human team managed to pull them open.

Five, who had been spinning faster and faster, and ratcheting itself down at the same time, released itself and sprang towards the enemy machines, who were by now all turned around in various directions, dazed and off-balance. As it flew, Five uncoiled multiple arms and gathered up the enemy machines and flew into the open elevator shaft, dropping them all the way down to the bottom.

Kat gasped. 'FIVE!' she yelled as the tall machine disappeared from sight through the elevator doors, and she gasped even louder as she saw Lewis run at full speed and slide over the threshold into the shaft. Lewis grabbed Artie as he slid, Artie grabbed Kat and Kat grabbed Eight. They all slid towards the almighty drop but suddenly stopped. Screeching sounds came from behind the line of machines and children as Thirty-Three, who had latched onto Eight, put itself into full reverse and hauled them back from the abyss.

Lewis re-emerged from the shaft with thin tendrils of uncoiled Tekktate wrapped around his legs and it was not long before they had pulled all of Five back up to safety. The machine had uncoiled significantly as it had plunged down the shaft - in an attempt to find some sort of purchase on the shaft walls or slow its descent - and it now more closely resembled the dishevelled mess of rootbranches Kat had first encountered.

The children gasped for breath and Eight hissed noisily from every joint as Five recoiled.

'Teamwork!' cried Artie, smiling and raising his hand skyward offering a high-five. Five itself had no idea what the gesture meant but it wanted to join in so slapped Artie's hand gratefully.

'That was very brave, Lewis,' said Kat, smiling at her panting brother.

'Foolish, more like,' said Artie sternly. 'The machine is still indestructible, you know!'

'Oh,' said Lewis, crestfallen. 'I forgot.'

'That also means those machines we just threw to the bottom of the tower won't be hurt,' said Kat. 'All we've done is buy ourselves some time.'

'They will be coming,' said Five.

'Or waiting,' said Artie. 'Assuming they can get through the elevator doors down there - we'll have to get past them again somehow.'

'It may take the machines a little longer than you think, Artie,' said Eight, ponderously. 'I do not believe that there are doors at the very bottom of the shaft - they will have to climb up a number of floors before they reach openings they can leave by. We must hurry if we are to avoid them.'

There was no debate this time and the group hot-footed it down the tower as fast as their legs, wheels and coils could take them. It was different now - they now knew there were machines awake outside of Time. Not simply Zero's followers as they had previously thought, but servants of another unknown and more powerful evil that could be anywhere. They somehow found more energy than they thought they had left in them; their speed increased when it should have slowed, spurred on by the need to avoid the awoken machines and the fear that there may be more. Their presence in Fabrakka was surely no longer a secret and they had lost any element of surprise they may have had.

Finally, they emerged from the same oddly-shaped doorway they had entered the tower by and without further incident. If the enemy machines had escaped from the shaft by now, they were nowhere to be seen - perhaps having returned to their Master.

'Way this,' said Thirty-Three as it shot off across the street. The group tried their best to keep pace with the wheel as it weaved around the polished streets and alleyways, taking the racing line wherever it could. Frequently though, Thirty-Three had to wait at a junction or corner for the band of stragglers to catch up.

'Now not far,' it said, looking around and getting its bearings. 'Where Five?'

The children looked around and realised that Five was no longer with them. Eight was hissing and wheezing from every seamless joint - the old hunched machine was obviously the slowest of the lot without two fully working legs. Surely Five was not slower than Eight?

'Wait here. Keep out of sight,' said Artie, and he slunk his way back through the alleyway and around the corner into the street.

It was some time before Artie returned, panting, and he looked very glum.

'It's done in,' he said. 'Completely frozen. No power... at all. I tried but I have... no green left. None of us do. No choice... but to just leave it...'

Lewis and Kat both looked at their hands. No green swam beneath the surface of their skin. Not only could they not see it, they could not feel it and they knew they had no excess power left inside them. All that was left was just enough to protect them from the ravages of no-Time.

Kat studied Eight.

Steam poured out of every invisible seam, the red charge around its damaged leg sparked furiously and the thin layer of red washing over the polished street clung ever more tightly to its feet. Even Thirty-Three's idling motor seemed more sluggish and was now sputtering.

She looked at the enormous, complex city that loomed all around them, washed completely in red Kora and her heart fell into her stomach.

She knew in that instant they were going to fail.

CHAPTER FOURTEEN

The Secret Facility

'Here,' said Thirty-Three, slowly trundling to a halt outside a comparatively nondescript building. They had made their way, as invisibly as they could, along a series of ever constricting alleys and narrowing, claustrophobic streets.

Kat looked around. This part of the city felt much smaller, with less grandeur and was certainly far, far older. She struggled to imagine any machine, large and suckered or tiny and diligent, spending any time here polishing the roads or sides of buildings. The area was not grubby or grotty by any stretch of the imagination, but it did not have the lustre of the resplendent area they had just left in a hurry.

They had not, thankfully, encountered any other machines since they had left Five, but that had only added to the feeling they were heading further into the boondocks of the city. The encounter with the enemy machines and the desertion of a helpless Five had left them feeling both frantic and glum.

'This area feels…' began Kat, '…oh, what's the word?'

'Obsolete?' said Artie.

'I was going to say abandoned…' she replied, '…but with machines, I guess obsolete is more accurate. What happened here?'

'Happened?' asked Eight. 'Nothing happened at all. This is the district of Tunkkaraa - we simply evolved other areas of the city over time to be... better. This area - quite a large area actually - is simply, as you have correctly stated, obsolete. It was closed down so that it could be regenerated. I believe work is due to begin relatively soon in fact. Every pillar, every pipe section, every duct, every bracket, every frame, every wire, every everything will be systematically stripped from top to bottom, sorted and evaluated. Those components that can be upgraded will be, and those components more suited to refactoring into something else entirely will be. Not a sliver of Tekktate will be wasted, and soon this district will be the new shining light of Fabrakka, towering above all other city districts. It is our way.'

'How long has it been left like this?' asked Lewis, looking around. 'I thought Fabrakkan machines would be so efficient and methodical that you could regenerate an area really very quickly.'

'It is true that we could,' replied Eight. 'The question is whether we *should*. Speed is not everything. A city in constant regeneration is not pleasant for those existing inside of it. The constant change, the inconvenience. Even we machines need to be able to live, and to appreciate the beauty of just living and enjoying what we already have. We could regenerate and evolve faster - far faster I am sure - but we would be collectively worse off for it.'

'How do we get in?' asked Artie, who had stopped listening to Eight and was studying the outside of the building. Although it looked very ordinary by Fabrakkan standards, Artie was starting to realise that the building had actually been fortified. A layer of robust but blank cladding had been added to the frontage of the building and covered every access point, window and opening. Except one.

'Yes,' said Thirty-Three, wheeling itself to the side of the doorway. 'Need code.'

Artie looked at the panel next to the only door. It did appear to be some kind of access terminal, although the functions of it looked entirely alien to him. This whole situation seemed odd to Artie - why fortify a building in an entirely peaceful world? Why require an access code in a world where trust is the only required currency?

'How does it work?' he asked the wheeled machine.

Horrid grinding noises emerged from Thirty-Three once more as it tried to access the files related to this building, but again could not.

'Not know,' the machine replied. 'Details unavailable.'

Artie rolled his eyes and sighed. He wanted to say something a little unkind to the obstructive machine but instead turned to Eight. 'Brute force?'

Eight ground out a short agreeable nod, and within just a few moments the children had taken cover in a nearby alleyway whilst Eight began the process of making another bomb. Thirty-Three remained nearby making encouraging sounds that Eight really could have done without.

The bomb was released, promptly exploded and Eight recoiled in the blast. Thirty-Three was sent rolling back across the street and had to put on its brakes to stop it hitting the buildings on the other side. Eight studied the door, which was now only partly dented and a little bent by the blast.

'Hmmm… disappointing,' mused the large machine as the children emerged from the alleyway and re-joined it at the door.

'Are you low?' asked Kat.

Eight grabbed the bent edge of the door and looked intently at it. 'Yes, unfortunately I am continuing to lose power due to the unexplained resistance - but I believe this door has also been reinforced. With a form of Tekktate that I am unfamiliar with. Fascinating. I will need to study this in more detail...'. Eight's swiss-army knife of tools began to emerge from its innards once more.

'We don't have time for a compositional analysis!' said Lewis, who was becoming more and more anxious at still being out in the open.

Eight's tools quickly disappeared back inside itself as it realised the boy was correct. Enemy machines could be upon them at any moment and they were very exposed in the streets.

'Help me,' said Artie as he grabbed an edge of the door. Soon, every child and machine had some sort of purchase on the entrance and were grunting, wheezing and hissing their way to making the small gap wider and wider. The distorted door scraped across the ground as they moved it, scratching and depressing the ground as it went.

Lewis and Kat disappeared into the building, followed by Thirty-Three. Eight looked at the marks made by the peculiarly strong door, as Artie watched the machine cross the threshold before stopping. 'That should not be possible,' thought the machine and instantly set a reminder in its internal chronometer to later complete the compositional analysis that Lewis had stopped it from performing.

The inside of the building was very dark - even if Time had allowed light to travel properly the interior would still be very dark due to all the covered openings. The group only had the dim lights of Eight and Thirty-Three's dials to see by.

'Next time on Fabrakka, I'm bringing a torch,' thought Kat, who had had enough of making her way through dark spaces. The first few rooms and corridors were small and entirely empty, but soon opened up into one large space - much like a very ordinary warehouse.

'Do you recognise this place, Thirty-Three?' asked Kat.

The wheel gently rolled back and forward. 'Yes. Here I have been. Delivering… <<<*NNNKKK*>>> cannot access records. Strange.'

Large containers were everywhere, stacked on top of each other, creating a whole new series of corridors. Something about the way that the large room was arranged seemed odd to Lewis and he could not quite put his finger on it at first.

'Of course…' he said eventually as his brain figured it out. 'Look at this… look at the way this container sits on this one. Not precise. Not organised. All higgledy-piggledy. As barking-mad as this city is, even the most twisted and complex of structures is perfectly calculated and precisely engineered. This is all sloppy, careless - not the work of machines!'

Eight's dials rotated and its lens zoomed in and out around the vast space made small and cramped by the plethora of containers - some closed, some open, but all messily arranged.

'I believe the boy is correct. Machines would not arrange a space like this. This is…'

'…disorganised,' said Kat finishing the machine's sentence.

Eight shook its head violently, its servos whirring aggressively. It lifted a component from one of the containers to show the group.

'Horrific!' said Eight, finishing its own sentence and discounting Kat's word. 'These containers are all filled with machine parts. Discarded. Unsorted. Unused. Wasted. Disrespected. Uncared for...'

'Maybe they just hadn't gotten around to it yet,' said Lewis. 'You said this whole area was due for regeneration...'

Eight's head had not stopped shaking. 'This is not the proper process,' it said, lifting the head-casing of an old machine in one hand, and a leg-brace in the other hand. 'No care has been taken here to properly evaluate each part. They have just been dumped. No machine would disrespect other machine parts like this.'

'That you know of...' said Lewis, whose mind had gone back to the control room machines, violated by whatever evil machine still lurked out there somewhere. He thought of what they themselves had done - removing the chipsets of the machines without their consent and realised that Eight was either being very naive or somewhat hypocritical.

'Look!' said Kat, as she reached an area with far fewer containers. A large bulbous structure stood on its own, under a cover made from a thin film of spun Tekktate. Kat ran her fingers across this new form of the wonder mineral before peeling it back to reveal the contents underneath. Lewis and Kat both gasped.

'It's...'

'...the machine that brought us here!'

'Or one just like it!'

'Except it's…'

'…kind of in bits.'

Like a partly completed jigsaw puzzle, the machine lay before them. In many ways it was identical to the machine in the mansion, but maddeningly incomplete. It seemed like most of the required parts were loosely stacked nearby, but it was impossible to tell if every required part was there. Kat moved to the underside of the machine to see if, just like in the mansion, there were symbols. The markings were there, and she called Eight across to translate them.

'P0-R7-4L [515] - 1/2,' read Eight aloud as its dials scanned and translated the symbols.

'1/2?' asked Lewis. 'What does that mean?'

'Usually when a machine is suffixed in that way…' said Eight, '…it is part of a set. This may be one of a pair.'

'The other in the mansion!' said Lewis. 'Are these machines linked? Could this machine take us straight back there?'

'Perhaps,' said Eight, scanning the pile of additional machine parts. 'More information is required. One wonders why the other machine did not bring you directly here to this place. Unless both machines need to be operating in tandem - synchronised in some form.' Eight looked at the incomplete machine. 'That may explain why you were only brought part-way and dumped in the wilderness.'

'Do you think this machine has been dismantled?' asked Kat. 'Or never even completed?'

'Again, impossible to tell without further information,' said Eight, very machine-like. 'If its construction was completed, we could ask it.'

'Ask it?' said Lewis and he realised the opportunity they had missed. 'We never thought to actually talk to the machine in the mansion. Why would we have?'

'We know better now,' said Kat. 'We've learned so much since then.'

'Indeed you have children,' said Eight. 'And accomplished much too. You have crossed the vast Fabrakkan wilderness, resurrected multiple machines along the way, disabled and disproven the threat that was Zero… and now, maybe you have found the link between our worlds.'

'Perhaps…' said Lewis, unconvinced that they had really achieved all that much, '…but without more green charge we are still stuck. Even rebuilding this machine would serve no purpose without it. Maybe Artie was right - maybe we do need to return to…'. Lewis stopped mid-sentence as he looked around and realised that Artie was not part of the group.

'Artie?'

Kat began to fret. She had known that something had been off with Artie ever since the control room, and she now began to worry that he had done something rash, perhaps even returning to the ocean all by himself and despite their deadly warnings.

'Artie!' they all called out in unison, as the band of machines and children began to search the container stacks - but there was no reply.

'When did you last see him?' Kat asked Lewis.

Lewis thought hard but struggled to remember clearly. 'The door? He helped us with the door, didn't he?'

Kat racked her brains. 'Yes… I think so - but I don't remember him saying anything after that. Did he even come inside the building with us?'

'I'm really not sure,' said Lewis glumly.

The group split apart and scoured the dark warehouse, looking for any sign of the missing boy. After a ruthlessly thorough, but unrewarding search, they came together as one to declare that Artie had truly gone.

'ARTIE!' Kat called out desperately once more.

Suddenly, from just beyond the stacks there came a series of sharp noises, and within just a few seconds the warehouse was filled with an army of machines, much like those they had encountered on their way back down the tower. Their many upper appendages had already been reconfigured, or in some cases, unsheathed - and the children, Eight and Thirty-Three stared at a vast array of sharp tools being wielded aggressively towards them.

'Kathra asta takka quix!' barked one of the machines, pointing its weaponized arm and glowing chest-plate directly at Eight's head casing.

Lewis gulped. 'What did it say?' he whispered to Eight, fearing that he already knew the answer. Eight's dials rotated and flickered uncontrollably, and the machine whirred and wheezed before replying.

'It said… we have you now!'

CHAPTER FIFTEEN

What Happened to Artie

'Then what would you suggest?' asked Artie, sulking a little. Neither Kat nor Lewis could offer a new suggestion and so Artie walked across to the large window by himself and looked over Fabrakka, stuck for an obvious way forward.

From the immense height of the control room, and with the partial but static cloud cover beneath, it was almost impossible to see anything at ground level clearly - except for the thin veils of red that were everywhere. Artie, however, stared intently at the streets below trying to figure out some sort of plan that did not involve potentially deadly risks like trekking all the way back to the ocean.

His eyes seared as an immense flash of green light suddenly exploded from the streets below. As soon as it had appeared, it was gone, and Artie initially questioned whether or not he had even truly seen it. He moved around the large panoramic window, trying to see if the bright green flash had simply moved away beneath the clouds, and before he knew it, he was in another part of the control room and the group were out of sight.

He was just about to call out to them, when instead Kat called out to him and then relayed Thirty-Three's offer to take them to the secret facility where a human had been seen long ago.

'Sounds like a reasonable idea,' he thought to himself. 'After all, did I really even see that green flash? Maybe I want to find more Kora so badly that I'm starting to imagine things...'

As the group made their way down the control tower, Artie realised he could not stop thinking about the green flash. He could sense that Lewis was, initially, calmer than usual but growing more on edge as they continued to descend the tower - but his concern for his friend seemed less important than finding out if the flash was real.

Even when they encountered the machines out of Time and all during the skirmish itself, he felt himself preoccupied by the green flash, drawn to it somehow. He tried to put it out of his mind and concentrate on helping the group find their way to the facility. When they realised Five had been lost, Artie volunteered to track back and find the tall machine in the hope that the flash had had something to do with Five's delay.

As they took cover from Eight's bomb, Artie finally made up his mind.

'All of this is for nothing if we have no green Kora,' he convinced himself. 'One by one the machines will fail, and we three will be stranded here forever with no way home and at the mercy of the enemy machines and whatever great destructive power that controls them.'

As they heaved the dented door open to allow access to the facility, Artie decided to slink away.

'Lewis and Kat will be fine with Eight and Thirty-Three, surely. I won't be gone long - it can't have been that far away. I'll run to where I saw the flash and if there's nothing there I'll run straight back. They won't even know I've gone. I'll barely be away five minutes. Maybe ten. Fifteen at the most. On my own I'm less likely to be seen. Even if I am, I can lure the enemy machines away from the group which will give them more chance to explore the facility safely. If I'm right, and there was a flash, we might have the means to restart the world - and then we can call upon an entire army of good machines to help us. What can we three children achieve by ourselves anyway?'

Before he knew it, he was running through the streets towards where he thought the green flash appeared. It was hard to be sure - all he had was a general compass direction - distances were difficult to precisely gauge from way, way up in the sky. However, he could feel the green pulling him towards it - he was close - he was sure of it.

He stopped in the middle of a wide street, having run without pausing, a stitch forming in his side and he was breathing hard. It was an empty street that they had not journeyed down previously, and he felt horribly exposed out in the open. There was something else - he could feel it all around him, something he had not felt for some time.

'A breeze!' he said to himself. 'I can feel the air!' It was swirling all around him, in its own little pocket, as though it had recently been disturbed. 'A breeze can only mean one thing…' he thought. 'Time!'

Artie spun around, on the spot, revelling in the free air - not horribly stale or oddly tasting as he had become used to. He stopped to think, but instead simply let the gently swirling air wash over him. He could somehow feel the residual green charge left in the air and knew where it led.

'This way, I think,' he said to himself as he followed the softly moving trail of air like a bloodhound. Being out in the open, exposed to the dangers of machines existing outside of Time, did not seem as important as following the trail - and Artie pursued it regardless of where it took him.

He lost track of how long he was away from the group. It could have been the five minutes, or the fifteen he had predicted, or more. He did not know, and he had stopped caring. This was the route he had to take - at the end of this trail lay the means to fix the world, to defeat the evil threat, to find the way home, to make everything better, everything right again like it used to be. Once or twice he thought he had lost the scent of the freely moving air, but he quickly found it again and realised that as he made his way along the air current, it became stronger and stronger.

'I must be getting closer to the source of whatever caused the green flash,' he thought. He considered the danger - what if the cause was not friendly? What if the cause was the great evil that controlled the machines? What did it matter? He would be careful, use more caution than he would normally, but the green must be pursued.

He snaked his way through the streets and alleyways. Occasionally he encountered a single, frozen machine and gave it as wide a berth as he could, trying not to be seen just in case a frozen machine was not truly frozen; simply pretending so that it could spy on trespassers in its upended world and either launch an attack or run off to find and recruit more comrades.

The trail led to a solid wall at the far end of a long, thin alleyway and disappeared. Artie's heart dropped into his stomach. He searched and searched all around for an offshoot of the trail -

another path to follow - but there was none. It just finished, in a literal dead end. He wiped away the water that had begun to escape his eyes and slumped to the ground, angry, defeated and desperately hurting.

He realised he had no idea how long he had been gone and decided that he had no other option but to return to the facility and regroup with the others. Maybe they had had better luck - maybe there was something in the facility that could help them all - some clue as to the professor's work. He suddenly grasped how foolish and reckless he had been to leave the others, without even telling them where he was going, or why he was leaving. Why did he not stay with them and search the facility? If there was nothing, he could then have told them all of the green flash and come here together. Maybe they could figure out how to recapture the trail and find out where it truly led? Why did he always rush in so blindly? He shook himself. He knew why and it was nothing to be ashamed of.

He stood up and a thought suddenly struck him. Back at the farm, there was an entrance, hidden in plain sight - covered by a contraption that only made it seem like there was nothing there. At least, that is how it should have worked. What if this was the same? Only working correctly. With renewed vigour he searched the wall again, pressing his hands against indistinct areas of smooth red-washed Tekktate, then moving to another patch and repeating. He stood back, calmed himself and let himself sense the trail of air. He found it with his heart, not his head, and reached out his hand and pushed into the precise spot on the wall. It resisted, then it gave slightly, and Artie fell through the solid wall that was now just an illusion.

He stood up in the darkened corridor and looked around. There was little to see, but there was light in the distance, and he carefully made his way towards it.

CHAPTER SIXTEEN

Power Extreme

Kat stepped in front of her brother, who had moved to do exactly the same thing at the same time and protect his sister. Eight however, had already altered its position to put itself between the children and the large group of enemy machines bearing down on them.

'What now?' said Kat, hoping that Eight was already in the process of making more bombs.

'I am afraid our options are, once again, very limited,' replied the machine. 'I am almost entirely out of power and it is unlikely that I can make more bombs with any destructive capability.' Eight's leg hissed and sparked violently with red and creaked in a way that suggested it was not long before the machine would no longer be able to stand. Eight looked at Thirty-Three forlornly. The little wheel revved in defiance, but the revs soon turned to splutters as it too realised it was desperately low on charge.

The enemy machine at the head of the large group raised its huge bulky arm and signalled to the other machines. Kat was unsure what the signal meant - were they about to be captured, or subjected to a deadly attack that they had no defence for? She thought she should close her eyes. Maybe it would not be so bad if she could not see it coming.

Suddenly from beyond the group of enemies there was a large clatter, then a loud noise that she instantly recognised, and the enemies were scattered like bowling pins as a furiously spinning Five careered across the warehouse, drilling its way through the pack and leaving a trail of intense green behind it.

Kat's heart leapt and her mouth dropped open as she saw what happened next.

Artie walked calmly across the warehouse. His tousled, spiky hair was taller and spikier than ever, and from the very bottom of his boots to the topmost strand of his hair he crackled with green power that enveloped him completely. He stood silently and calmly assessed the situation, before unleashing huge arcs of green Kora from his fingertips in every direction. He hit Eight directly in the chest-plate and the green charge lit up all its dials. An arc of green travelled from its head-casing down its blackened body towards its damaged leg and burrowed its way inside. In the next second a flurry of red charge was furiously expelled from its leg, exploding into nothingness, and the machine's parts snapped themselves back together as good as new. Green hit and flooded Thirty-Three and its wheel spun more and more furiously, the green charge becoming whiter and whiter as it picked up speed and revved deafeningly.

More and more strands of blinding, intense green power left Artie, this time hitting Lewis who was lifted off his feet on a cushion of green charge that then flooded every part of him from bottom to top. Kat did not have time to react as a second strand hit her, and she felt the wonderful sensation of being raised off the floor and welcomed back the illuminating power that she had so sorely missed. She was once again, at one with Fabrakka, empowered by the precious element of this fantastical world and her heart almost burst with devotion.

The enemy machines did not know which way to turn or what to do. No matter where they looked, there was a machine, or a fleshbot, flooded with such blindingly bright power they could not cope with it. It did not matter what plan of attack they had, or could formulate in a thousand instant internal processes, for they had no defence for what Artie did next.

As simply as gently shrugging, Artie shook off the green. For a second he was just Artie, but then he clenched his fists together and everything changed. Red Kora completely enveloped him, fizzing and crackling all over his body and his eyes flared devilishly. His hair, even taller this time, shot red arcs upwards and all around - and from his palms, huge ruby-red lightning bolts burst in every direction. Every enemy machine, in a single instant, was frozen to the spot as a perfectly aimed arc of red power hit them and trapped them in the frozen wasteland of Time.

Again, Artie shrugged it all off as naturally as taking a breath and lowered himself gently to the floor. The red dissipated and Artie emerged from the mass of energy, just a young boy from a tiny village once more.

Kat rushed to Artie and flung her arms around his neck and repeatedly kissed his cheek. Then she took a step backwards and punched him hard and square in the chest.

'Don't ever leave me like that again!' she yelled, before again throwing her arms around him and hugging him tightly.

Thirty-Three wheeled around Artie in delight, Five sprung around the group in a giddy circle of babbling voices, and Eight strode purposefully across to the boy, who was now clutching and rubbing his sore, bruised chest.

'You have some explaining to do,' said Eight, sternly.

Artie nodded and told them his story.

*

He stood up in the dark corridor and looked at the dim light at the far end. Behind him, there was again a series of pipes that wrapped itself around the invisible entrance, just like at the farm. However, the design of the fully functioning concealed entrance, and the security machine a short distance away, was more elegant, more refined, but undeniably similar.

'The professor's lab!' he thought. 'It must be…'

He cautiously walked along the corridor, convinced that the flash of green and the trail of swirling air was the wake of Professor Alexander who had perhaps just journeyed back to Fabrakka from their own world.

'Or perhaps another world entirely!' thought Artie, and the idea that there were even more worlds out there, more possibilities, filled him with great excitement and hope. He came to the end of the corridor, where it turned slightly before opening up into a modestly sized but impressively stuffed laboratory.

There were contraptions everywhere. Half-built machines were scattered across the entire place. In one area, there was a large workbench and across it there were hundreds of individual samples of Tekktate in all manner of different forms and sizes. Great big solid coarse lumps, piles of loose dirt-but-not-dirt, twisted spun strands, smooth slivers, cut shards and transparent prisms, and sheets that were so thin it was hard to know if they were even truly there. They were all individually labelled and appeared to have been sorted and categorised, but Artie did not recognise any of the symbols - he was not even sure if the language was Fabrakkan. Various tools of the kind that Artie had never seen were placed all around the samples. They looked like every one of Lewis' father's engineering tools combined into one implement, and then many more unique variations besides. What they were all for, he could not comprehend.

Artie wondered if, amongst all the half-built machines, there were any that were sentient. The whole laboratory was eerily silent, but amongst all the machinery and parts and dark corners anything could be lurking. He thought he should call out, to let them know that he was there, that he was human, a friend in need of help - but he kept silent. Something held him back. As he looked at the incomplete machines a dark thought crossed his mind. What if these machines were not half-built? What if they were half-dismantled? What if this was not the professor's lab at all, but something else's entirely? What if this was the lair of the great evil that had corrupted so many machines and could exist completely outside of Time? What if he was in danger, right now? He could not be alone in here - the trail of air he had followed had clearly been made by something that led him to this place and was surely still here, somewhere in the shadows. He was just about to hide so that he could observe whatever it was without being detected, when he turned and saw it.

At the far end of the laboratory, on a raised platform, was a large machine unlike any other he had seen so far. In the centre, it was round - a flawless sphere and polished black like the most perfectly pure and refined Tekktate always is. Great wiry strands spat out of the sphere on either side, like a thousand flailing arms and they all connected to one of two things. On one side there was a tall transparent tube filled with pulsing green Kora, and on the other side another tube filled with the crackling red charge.

Thoughts of hiding quickly left his mind as he approached the machine and stepped up onto the platform. The green inside the tube reacted to his presence - it changed its shape and flow and followed his every movement. He walked all around the machine, looking for the symbols that could provide a clue as to the machine's purpose. Even though he could not read Fabrakkan, something inside told him he would be able to grasp their meaning. Surprisingly, there were no symbols he could see, and he emerged from the far side of the machine. The red in the tube also reacted to him, but not by moving as the green did. It intensified in colour and brightness and Artie felt as though it was transfixed on him - perhaps even studying him, deciding if he was good or evil. If he could be trusted. If he was the one.

Artie felt uncomfortable and took a step backwards away from the glaring intensity of the red, and that was when it happened. In a split second, two tiny openings appeared in the tubes and both green and red tendrils shot simultaneously from them, grabbing Artie, wrapping all around him and wrestling him to the ground. He screamed - not in pain for it was entirely painless - but in shock at the incredible sensations that now swept up and down his convulsing body. As soon as it had begun it ended, and Artie lay panting on the ground.

He stood up ungainly - his body still shaking, before coming to a perfect, calm state. He opened his eyes and smiled, and now knew exactly what needed to be done.

*

'An extraordinary story,' said Eight. 'One filled with worrisome developments. Another facility, in plain sight and right under our centrally positioned air filters.'

Kat and Lewis exchanged confused glances until they both realised that Eight meant noses. Perhaps the pompous machine was finally developing a sense of humour - but it hardly seemed the time for it.

'Worrisome, maybe...' said Artie confidently, '...but we now have enough green to restart Time, and I have enough red to freeze any machines that challenge us. So, what are we waiting for?'

CHAPTER SEVENTEEN

A World Unstuck

Kat laid her right hand gently on the panel next to the doors to call the service elevator down to them. She had been looking forward to this moment - to use the green Kora that was again coursing inside her - for the good of all the group.

CLANG! CLANG!

The doors jerked open and Kat recoiled as she came face to face with three enemy machines wielding their razor-sharp tools. One of the machines took a wild swing - which would have connected with her head had it not frozen mid-swipe. Kat turned to see Artie, flaming red, with tendrils of red Kora wrapped around his arms calmly reeling in his enemies. He then extended himself, and the machines were flung through the doors from whence they came - back down to the bottom of the elevator shaft they had just finished clambering up, moments ago.

Kat's hard breathing eased, and the group's attention was interrupted by a familiar voice and space that had now descended into their line of sight.

'Oh, hello again,' said the elevator cheerily. 'Where to this time?'

*

Eight studied the layout of buttons, dials, switches, levers and various other sockets and interfaces of the control desk.

'If you would be so kind, children,' it said and gestured towards the large desk. Kat laid both her hands on the desk and let a small amount of green flow out of them. Several lights blinked on, various knobs gently rotated automatically, and rocker switches flicked back to their default positions.

Eight contemplated the new layout, before clapping its bulky clamp-hands together, somewhat gleefully.

'I believe I now have the correct sequence. When I give the signal, unleash as much Kora as you can and I will, hopefully, reactivate all of the control tower's systems.'

Eight flicked a series of switches, rotated the first, second then third dial, and pulled the largest of levers.

'Now!' it said authoritatively.

All three children positioned themselves and let loose their charge - the desk erupted in crackling green energy as Eight pushed and released the large button - the same one that had once been directly under Zero's brutish hand. The machine was now placed to one side of the desk, vacantly observing the undoing of its enforced work. Artie watched Kat and Lewis as they generously, almost completely, emptied themselves of all their positive power, and he guiltily withdrew his hands from the desk, knowing that he could not help but hold himself back a little.

All around them, the thin red veils dissipated, chased away by tendril after tendril of green Kora that spread and spread and spread as far as they could see, becoming an enormous, unstoppable wave as it went. As it travelled, it too changed - affected by the control tower's now active systems, becoming less verdant and much paler - before evolving into a shimmering silver film that was now everywhere. As it washed over every part of the world, Fabrakka changed beyond all recognition. Every surface burst with intensely vibrant colour - as if some unseen entity had remotely turned the colour dial on a television to maximum. Every perfectly polished surface somehow managed to look even cleaner and brighter and glistened in the light of the three suns that rose fully, scattering light everywhere. The air around them swirled once more and the children could again breathe deeply and fully - the horrid stale taste had been replaced with something subtly, deliciously sweet. There was a low gentle, soothing rattle and hum that came from everywhere - the sound of great machinery once again in action. It pulsed rhythmically, and the world felt as though it had a tangible heartbeat and was fully alive once more. From outside the large window of the control room, there came a different noise. The bustling world of Fabrakka below had resumed and they could all hear the everyday hubbub of hundreds of machines again going about their mechanised lives.

Those machines nearby carried on as though nothing had ever been wrong, but the machines outside the centre of the city stopped and took time to understand what had possibly happened. Everything was ok, then it had begun to be confusing and then... then... Many of them decided to reboot their systems or perform a quick low-level defragmentation to shake off the feeling that the world had been briefly faulty. The machines at the very outskirts of the city, however, rejoiced as they understood that the broken world had once again been fixed by some unknown force that they had to find and congratulate and thank.

Kat looked around the control room which was, like everything else, swimming in glistening colour. The atmosphere was entirely different than before, and yet her eyes were drawn to and rested on the still frozen machines scattered around the room - those machines whose casings had been violated and whose chipsets had been removed. They served as a reminder that although the world had been unstuck, it could never again be just as it was before. Eight had walked across to the girl, sensing her inner turmoil and joined her in staring at the static vacuous machines that now seemed even odder in a world where Time flowed freely once more.

'Our world is restored, thanks to you. It has, however, been forever altered.'

'The threat is still out there, somewhere. Whatever it is,' sighed Kat.

Eight nodded and rotated its dials so that the compass-like dial was at the top. 'Yes. There is much still to be done. Much to be discussed and perhaps, debated. There is a small group of machines, a commune that resides in Kasperitakk and have existed for longer than most machines in this world. They have resisted the need to change - at least, they have resisted change at the rapid pace of the many newer machines, and yet they have also resisted obsolescence. I will go there and consult with them on how to move this world forward. These frozen machines - we must find out which of them were complicit in the plan to break the world; determine which of them are to be punished or merely admonished and set free. They are to be pitied - if it is found that they were corrupted and used unwittingly. We will have to establish some form of fair process - some means to uncover the truth and reach a justice that serves all machines. Without crime, there was no need for punishment on Fabrakka. Now we have both - but in doing so we may also discover what this great threat is, and what it wants. We have restored the world, but the red Kora cannot now be uninvented. It may find a way to return, if that is the will of the evil that hides in some corner of our now vulnerable world.'

'And then you will stop it?' asked Kat.

Eight nodded and pulled the many chipsets from one of its hidden compartments. The machine stared at them, but Kat could not bring herself to look at the immobilised minds of the machines that sat dumbly in Eight's hulking clamp-like palm.

'Our part in this will not be glossed over,' said Eight glumly. 'I may find that some form of my own punishment is necessary, if all is to be appeased. But what happens now is for the machines of Fabrakka to resolve. Our focus now must be in returning you children home - I shall instruct a specialist group of machines to begin reconstructing the machine we uncovered at the facility. Hopefully it is what we believe it to be, and it can send you all back to your own world.'

Kat nodded - and inside she desperately wanted to go home - but the words that escaped her mouth betrayed that. 'Oh, not yet,' she said, pressing herself against the panoramic window and looking down beneath the now shifting clouds. 'We want to finally see Fabrakka as it should be. As much of it as we can!'

Lewis joined his sister at the window, and Artie, Five and Thirty-Three also came closer to reform the group of heroes. The noise below them was growing louder and there seemed to be, even at this immense height, no escape from the commotion below.

'Very well, then,' said Eight. 'We should go and spread the word that this world owes a great debt to our human friends.'

*

'Who-man?' said one of the machines. 'What is a who-man?'

'Not who-man!' said another. 'Human.'

'How is that different? These new words are very unclear.'

Eight had stood on the steps at the entrance to the control tower and addressed the crowd of machines that had gathered; some had been very confused and some very excited. Amongst themselves they had discussed the situation and it was generally accepted that something had broken the world and it was probably very dangerous for a while, but it had seemingly all been resolved thanks to the two machines and three fleshbots standing beside the machine that was talking to them all. Every machine's internal chronometer was reading differently and so there was much checking what the time was and resetting and rebooting of various systems. Eight explained that the green charge that had restored the world had come directly from the children, and as a result each machine may find that they knew certain things they did not know before and that they had access to a new, very colourful and imprecise language. There were many humorous exchanges between the machines as they tried out their new skills, but then Eight's address turned to darker topics.

'We must be vigilant!' cried Eight loudly. 'In this world, there is now a force that means to do us harm. We do not know what it is, or where it is… or even what it wants. We do know that it exists and has the power to corrupt and control us.'

A great mechanical muttering spread across the crowd, and Eight heard a small number of loud disbelieving and dissenting voices amongst the chatter and clanging.

'This could be far more difficult than I anticipated,' said Eight.

*

Over the next several hours, Eight, Five and Thirty-Three took great delight in showing the children more of the great city. Kat could not wait to ride the whalebus, whose designation was W4-R8-LR, and she laughed as it swooped and dived around the spires of many twisted buildings whilst singing its percussive, banging whalesong. Eight introduced the children to many more machines, who were only too eager to meet the who-mans and understand what made them so special.

There was 5T-R3-CH, the (very polite) telescopic ladder-like machine they had noticed earlier propped up against the side of a building, and whose primary function was to allow the very smallest of machines to more quickly access the upper floors. There was also FL-1N-6R, a transportation machine (not unlike a giant waddling catapult), whose special spun strands of webbed Tekktate were extraordinarily pliable. It offered to propel the children to any part of the city they wished to go to and was very surprised to learn that the children were not indestructible and would not survive the landing.

'How do you ever get anywhere?' it asked rhetorically before shuffling off to assist other machines in need of unnecessarily speedy and reckless travel.

Kat paused to look up at the buildings that loomed tall over them and realised that everything now seemed to be moving all at once. It was not just the fact that they were glinting in the light, reflecting it in ways that her eyes could properly understand - the entire city now seemed to be behaving like one great harmonious and perfectly functioning engine. She saw the spiderpillar weave another balustrade; it was moving at the fast speed she was expecting - but it did not craft one balustrade and then another and another - it spun just one, then beavered away at its creation, engineering and refining it with such incredible precision and care that belied the enormous machine that had made it.

Kat looked down as she felt a very pleasant rubbing sensation on one of her legs and was delighted to see the tiny street-polishing machine she had spoken to when they first arrived in the city. It was very quiet, seemingly shy and whispered its designation, 6R-00-MR. It hopped up onto Kat's shoulder and began to polish her dark red hair, trying to restore its usual lustre that had become dulled by all their adventures. Kat enjoyed the sensation so much that she let 6R-00-MR ride around on her shoulders as they continued to tour the immense, bustling, now gleaming technicolour-washed city.

They soon met some machines whose functions were a little harder for the children to appreciate. There was 45-50-RT; a jolly, bulky machine that would reconfigure any combination of machine parts into any other random combination in the hope that something uniquely special and unthought-of would emerge from its innards. The machine was cube-shaped and split up into multiple parts and reminded Artie of a coloured puzzle where you had to line up all the same colours together to solve it. Eight, explained that, to date, 45-50-RT had yet to reconfigure any parts into a machine that served any useful purpose - and it had so far produced 426,713 unique combinations.

'Maybe next time will be the one, though!' it chuckled as the children said a bemused goodbye.

PL-UK-3R was just as baffling to the children. It hovered slightly above the ground and, like Eight, had a toolkit of bizarre little devices at its disposal. It explained that its primary function was to remove imperfections from Tekktate. Kat thought that was a very worthy premise, but soon changed her mind when PL-UK-3R explained that it had been searching for over a hundred cycles and had yet to find a single imperfection anywhere in the city.

'Oh,' said Kat, unsure at first of what to say. 'Maybe you will have to go further afield to find what you are looking for.' The idea of leaving the city had never occurred to this particular machine, and it wandered off muttering to itself about who-mans and their very odd, radical ideas.

'Don't get me wrong,' whispered Lewis to Artie after they had encountered another host of baffling machines that had made both their heads spin. 'I love this world. It's completely bonkers. But aren't some of these machines... well, *pointless*?'

Despite keeping his voice as low as he could, Eight had overheard Lewis and could not help but interject.

'Fabrakkans do not judge how any other machine chooses to be. We understand that what may seem like a frivolous machine today, may evolve into one with the most important function in a hundred or a thousand cycles from now. We let each machine decide for itself its own destiny and to find its own place in the world - however long that may take. Besides, it is in our nature to build, to construct; often we tinker and experiment for our own amusement and leisure. It is as natural to us as breathing is to you.'

'That's... I guess... a nice way to look at it,' agreed Lewis, feeling slightly humbled.

The children were all starting to feel weary and hunger was growing strongly within them as Eight introduced them to two more machines; R3-L4-Y5 was a sort of public broadcast system whose job it was to spread serious newsworthy events. However, the world being frozen was the first major crisis that had ever happened on Fabrakka, and with it being frozen, R3-L4-Y5 had missed the entire thing until it was too late to tell anyone anything.

'My future purpose lies elsewhere,' it said unhappily. 'I am clearly not specialised enough to perform these operations and serve Fabrakka as I should. I may journey to Kasperitakk and reconsider my primary function.'

The children realised that many more of the machines felt that way as a result of the time-freeze they were helpless to prevent. W4-TC-HR was the patrol machine, whose job was to scour the city and report anything that was not quite right or identify areas most in need of regeneration. It was this machine that had first noticed the barriers being quickly erected and groups of machines suddenly gathering suspiciously in odd places at odd times.

'But when it came to it...' said W4-TC-HR, '...I was unable to do anything useful to stop events unfolding as they did. It all happened too fast. I, too, will go to Kasperitakk and think on what my future function should be. And my form too - I have always had a strong liking for the colours pink and green together. Perhaps a repainting will help me feel better - there is much too much blackness everywhere for my liking. Hmmm... spots or stripes?'

*

'It is time, children,' said Eight. 'I have received word that the machine is nearing full reconstruction. We should return to the facility and attempt to send you home; by the time we get there, it will be complete.'

'Good,' said Artie bluntly as he munched wearily on a dry Tekktate biscuit that Eight had recently prepared for the weakening children. 'If I don't get any real food soon, I think I'll scream.'

Kat turned red and her eyes began to, ever so slightly, water.

'Our parents…' she said, '…they'll be worried sick. We just vanished. Have we been gone for days or weeks? It's so hard to tell with Time all messed up. Lewis must feel as though he's been away for months.'

Lewis nodded and Artie could see that he was also turning a little red in his gaunt cheeks, but the boys stayed silent.

The children, Eight, Five and Thirty-Three began to make their way towards the no-longer-secret facility. The journey was not particularly long, but along the way, the Fives became involved in yet another internal debate. There was much low muttering before the words became clear.

'You ask it…'

'…no, you.'

'Why me?'

'…because you noticed it!'

'Oh… ok then.'

'Erm, Eight... we were wondering... what seems to be wrong?'

Eight's dials narrowed and spun, and it seemed to be eyeing the tall machine with suspicion. Before it replied, however, its dials widened and calmed as it realised Five had in fact been very perceptive.

'I am not sure, my friend. Ever since we restored Time, I have sensed that something is different with the world. Something is not quite right - it has not returned to the exact state it was before Time froze. I have reset and recalibrated my internal chronometer more than once, and yet it does not seem to be tracking correctly. Something remains... off.'

'We have all been through quite the adventure,' said Five. 'It may be some time before all of our systems return to normal.'

'True,' said a Five.

'Too true,' said another.

'Perhaps...' said Eight. 'I am not convinced that it is all that simple. Only the passing of Time, and perhaps a fuller suite of diagnostic checks, will inform us.'

Before too long, the group had re-entered the facility and made their way to the place where the strange machine had been. It looked quite different now that it had been fully rebuilt, and it was almost (but not quite) identical to the one in the mansion.

'How does it operate, children?' asked Eight.

The children looked at one another exchanging confused glances. Artie shrugged.

'No idea,' he said. 'We didn't do anything to start it up as far as we know. It just... came alive.'

'Fascinating...' said Eight. 'Well, perhaps we can ask it?'

Eight tapped its bulky hand on the polished black outer casing of the machine, as if it was knocking at a door.

'Hello?' it asked. There was no reply.

'Perhaps a jump start?' said Eight, gesturing to the children.

'Oh, let me,' pleaded Kat. 'I think I still have enough left.'

She laid her hands gently on the machine and let the green charge leave her. The tendrils of Kora worked their way all over the machine and soon many dials flickered, and multiple bulbs illuminated.

'Where... am I?' asked the machine.

'You are on Fabrakka,' replied Eight. 'Does that mean anything to you?'

'Well of course it does,' said the machine. 'I am Fabrakkan. I meant where in the great city am I? I do not recognise this facility. Where is the professor?'

'Ah. So Professor Alexander did build you?' asked Lewis, who had of course read about these machines in the professor's notebook.

'If you mean the tall, thin fleshbot with strange white hair, yes - it built me. Not much for talking though that one. I always had the feeling that it did not like me all that much. That I was something of a disappointment to it. Where is my brother?'

'Your brother?' asked Five, unsure of the machine's meaning.

'I think it means the other machine - the one from the mansion,' said Lewis.

'Yes, my brother - designation P0-R7-4L [8R0] - 2/2. We were to be reunited, according to the fleshbot. Next thing I know, darkness, then I am here speaking to you, somehow, in this new language. Can we not speak Fabrakkan rather than these inaccurate linguistic exchanges?'

Eight sighed mechanically. 'Can you help us?' it urged. 'We need to return these children to their own world. We believe it was your brother that sent them here.'

'Oh,' said the machine. 'Well, that changes things, I guess. Let me see if I can connect to my brother...'

P0-R7-4L [515] - 1/2 whirred and clunked and hummed, as though it was thinking very hard. In fact, it was trying to reach out beyond this world through the invisible network of energy lines that ran across Fabrakka and into other worlds.

'No answer,' it said. 'However, I can certainly return you to your world. If I could connect to my brother, I would be able to send you to its exact location. Without that connection I am not sure quite where you will end up, but I have sent the quiet, thin fleshbot to its world many times. Is it the same world you wish to travel to?'

The children nodded and shouted 'YES!' all together as they understood that they were truly about to return home and finally put an end to their parents' pain.

'Ok then,' said the machine, spinning up. 'Get ready!'

With those words Kat realised that it really was now time to say goodbye to Eight, Five and Thirty-Three. The tears she had fought hard to suppress earlier could not be held back this time - but she was not alone. Lewis and Artie were both fighting to keep their emotions in check.

'We wish you safe travels, eternal Heroes of Fabrakka,' said Eight. 'You will always be welcome in this world. You have earned the right to forever be part of it.'

'Absolutely,' said Five.

'Look us up,' said Thirty-Three.

Kat rushed to Eight and threw her arms around the bulky machine. Her arms could not wrap all around it - not even close - but it was the best hug she could manage. Eight understood and returned the hug by very gently squeezing her. Five uncoiled multiple arms and shook all three children's hands at the same time. Thirty-Three sped all around them, darting in and out of the children like an excited puppy, even though it also felt sad to be saying goodbye.

The beam of light spun out of the machine. Lewis noticed that it behaved quite normally this time; the few small particles that were caught inside the beam were not frozen as they had been inside the mansion - they danced rapidly around in a frenzy. Eight studied their dancing patterns, and the speed they were moving at, and as the white circle of light grew and enveloped the children, Eight finally understood what was now wrong with the world.

The children waved goodbye to their friends as Fabrakka started to blur. Kat could see Eight waving back, but it was no longer a friendly wave - it was moving its arms frantically, and seemed to be signalling to them to stop, to come back... to return to Fabrakka? Kat was unsure of the machine's meaning, and as everything continued to blur, she caught fragmented glimpses of words.

'...Time - not reset...'

'...faster, faster...'

'...danger...'

'...help...'

'...too FAST!'

Kat felt the same pull she had when the mansion machine had transported them to Fabrakka. She steeled herself, half-expecting the world around to both implode and explode at the same time, just as the mansion had done. This time, though - it was different. Their friends, the machines, zipped away at an incredible speed and then the walls and roof of the facility, section by section, systematically deconstructed allowing the children to see outside. The streets beyond, earmarked for regeneration were torn down and replaced in seconds, and every building around was deconstructed and rebuilt as far bigger and far grander, again in the blink of an eye. The blurring intensified and then there were multiple great flashes of light; as the light dimmed slightly, they could see that they were huge explosions; shattering everything nearby and an enormous shockwave boomed its way towards them.

Before it hit them, everything spun dizzyingly and went completely dark.

CHAPTER EIGHTEEN
Three Children and The Pact

The air smelled damp and musty, and the children - who had been holding their breath - finally let go and breathed deeply, taking it in. Once more, darkness surrounded them, and their fuzzy eyes took time to adjust to the very limited light.

'Is everyone ok?' asked Artie. Kat was, at first, unsure and so she both nodded and shook her head at almost the same time. As she slowly realised that she was unhurt, and could breathe without issue, the nodding increased and the shaking lessened.

'Dirt,' said Artie, bending down and running the loose ground through his fingers. 'Actual, dirty dirt. I think we're home. But… where are we?'

The children looked around the darkness. It felt close in the cramped dark place they now found themselves in.

'It feels like a cave,' said Kat running her hands along the rough wet wall.

'It looks like a cave,' said Lewis, squinting towards the small crack of light in the distance that made the space not just pure blackness.

'It's a cave,' said Artie firmly. 'Strange, though. I didn't know there were any caves near our village. Come on.'

As they walked slowly, being very careful where they tread, Lewis spoke to say what had been on all of their minds since everything stopped spinning.

'What *was* that?' he asked. 'Did you both see the same as I did? The world moving so fast it became a total blur? The structures - torn down in a second and rebuilt in another? The... explosions?'

'I saw the same,' said Artie glumly.

'Me too,' said Kat.

'What does it mean?' asked Lewis, his voice now wavering and breaking.

'I'm worried,' said Kat, shaking her head. 'Eight... Five... Thirty-Three. All of them. What if they were caught in those explosions?'

'What if they really aren't indestructible anymore?'

'What if we didn't really fix the world?'

'What if we did fix Time, but have somehow made it even worse?'

'Eight was trying to tell us something as we left.'

'Trying to stop us...'

'Trying to warn us? Of what?'

Kat screamed through the darkness as something at her feet suddenly moved and rattled. Artie gestured to her and Lewis to stay as still as they could as he slowly bent down to see what it was.

It was a skeleton.

Its clothes were so ragged and torn and fragile that when Artie touched them, they crumbled at the edges and frayed to almost nothing. There was no flesh left on it at all, but its thin hair was wild and very long. The bones of its feet poked through what little was left of its shoes. Lewis and Kat took a full step backwards away from the horrible sight as Artie bravely peeled back the decaying layers of what seemed to be very old but formal clothing and rummaged in the faded blazer pocket looking for clues.

'What are you doing?' whispered Lewis, rather disturbed at the sight.

Artie did not answer, but instead gently lifted an item from the inside pocket and carefully opened it. It was a wallet, covered in dust and bits of some other things Kat did not want to know. Artie, as gently as he could, blew away and shook off the dust before opening the tatty wallet fully.

The first thing he lifted out was a small piece of card, but it was so faded and so fragile that it simply turned to dust in his hands. The second thing he lifted out was similar in size but a little sturdier and was covered in some sort of resin that had stopped it from fading or crumbling fully. He turned it over - there was an image - and as he saw it, his face fell.

'Professor James Bartholomew Alexander,' he said gloomily. 'Born October 21, 1872.'

'Died a very, very, very long time ago by the looks of it,' said Lewis, trying not to be sick.

'He never made it home,' said Kat forlornly, now looking down directly at the skeleton that had initially scared her so much. 'Not all the way. The poor, poor man.'

Artie stood up, thinking - but did not voice out loud the thoughts he now had. The professor was dead - and had been for many decades. If it was not the professor he had followed on Fabrakka, who was it? What was it? More possibilities flooded his mind, but he kept them to himself and simply said:

'Come on. Let's get out of this cave and see where we have landed.'

The cave snaked and twisted for quite a while. Every now and then a crack in the roof let in a new shaft of light and gave them more false hope that they were nearing an exit. They were starting to become very weary when a small chink of light became a larger shaft which then became a flood, and they stood at the opening to the cave on a hillside looking down at their very own village.

'I had no idea this cave was here,' said Artie. 'I thought I'd been everywhere in this village.'

Lewis stood, mouth open, pointing at a large building off to one side in the distance. 'Look!' he yelled.

The mansion was there, fully intact, as though nothing had happened to it at all.

'I don't understand,' he continued. 'If the mansion is fine, then maybe... maybe Fabrakka is fine. Maybe all that stuff we saw as we moved between worlds was all in our heads.'

'Maybe travelling like that warps our minds,' said Artie. 'Maybe they can't fully understand what's happening to our bodies, so it makes stuff up in our heads to try to explain it?'

'So the mansion didn't collapse...' said Kat, '...and maybe Fabrakka didn't explode or even speed up? Maybe everyone is fine?'

'Maybe...' said Artie, '...but we'd need to know for sure - not knowing will eventually drive us all mad. It's vital we find out if everyone is safe. First things first though - we need to get home.'

'Our parents...' said Lewis, choking and unable to find the rest of the words. The thought of what their parents were going through hit him like a truck and he realised that nothing else mattered right now except telling them that everything was fine. That they were all fine.

The three children ran as fast as they ever had through the thin, narrow streets of their small village, which now felt smaller than ever. They reached the front gate of Lewis and Kat's garden and stopped, nodded to each other and sped up the path to the front door as Artie ran on towards the garden immediately next door.

'We're ok, we're ok!' yelled Kat as the twins burst into the hallway - the front door clattering and rebounding off the wall.

'Katherine Edith Crawford!' came an angry voice from another room. Her father emerged from the kitchen; his arms covered in soapy suds from the washing up. 'Lewis Andrew Crawford! You are nearly thirty minutes past your curfew!'

'Thirty minutes?' blurted Kat, bewildered.

Her father sighed loudly, but his stern expression did not change. 'This is Arthur's fault, again, isn't it? Off chasing dragons today or some such, were we? That boy and his imagination! Honestly... the three of you live in each other's pockets so much these days you're practically becoming one person. Now, look at me! What's the rule?'

'Don't leave the village and don't miss curfew,' said Lewis automatically.

'Bed! Now!' yelled their father, who was so tired and angry he had not even absorbed Lewis' dishevelled, thin appearance.

Kat tried hard not to lose control of her emotions, and she just about held it all back as they made their way upstairs. Confusion and (mostly) relief washed over her, and she hugged her brother tightly as they realised the immense pain that they had imagined their parents to be drowning in had never existed at all. But she still did not entirely understand.

*

'I'm back, mum!' said Artie as he opened the front door. The painting on the wall did not respond - she never did - but Artie spoke to her as he ran across the hallway, just like always.

'You won't believe the day I've had,' he said to her in passing as he reached the bottom step of the large staircase.

'Arthur?' came a soft voice from the next room. 'Don't disturb him. Not now.'

Artie ignored the voice and continued to run up the many stairs and did not slow down until he had reached the large imposing door at the far end of the upper hallway. He turned the handle gently, as slowly as he could, and slid quietly through the small gap into the dark room.

The air was so stale he found it hard to breathe. The room was almost completely dark, as it always was. The silence was almost total, except for the regular beeping of the machine and the measured rise and fall of the mechanical breathing.

'Dad?' he said, softly.

There was no response, and Artie approached the side of the bed and gently sat next to his father.

'Dad?' he asked again, with more intensity.

The eyes flickered slightly underneath the pale eyelids but did not open. The voice struggled.

'Arthur?'

'I'm here,' said Artie.

Artie lifted his father's hand and grasped it tightly. He closed his own eyes and relaxed as much as he could. He could feel himself emptying - the green Kora left him in a gentle, regular flow. The guilt he had felt for holding some back in the control room washed over him again, but quickly disappeared as he felt the changes unfold in front of him. He opened his eyes to see his skin sparkle with a small, thin burst of green tendrils, then fade to nothing as they travelled from him into his father. He looked at his father's pale face and saw the colour returning to his cheeks and his closed eyes darting back and forth. His lips blossomed with red and the air around him brightened, for a second or so, before being swamped once more with the cruel staleness. Soon, his lips paled, the cheeks sunk, the eyes beneath the lids calmed once more and his father's laboured breathing returned.

Artie hung his head, wiped the tears from his eyes and left the dark room to go downstairs and talk to the nurse.

*

THUNK! SCHLUK!

Lewis knew exactly what the sound meant and rushed to the bedroom window and opened it. He reached round and pulled the plastic dart suckered to the glass pane away. He brought it inside and unwrapped the scrawled note crudely attached to the dart with string and tape.

'Meet outside mansion - 8am. A,' he read aloud to Kat.

Kat nodded, the smile spreading widely across her freckled face.

*

'Thanks mum!' yelled Lewis as he wolfed down the last spoonful of breakfast cereal (third helping) and threw his empty bowl in the sink. Kat copied her brother, grabbed her school bag and barged her way past her father who had stumbled to the bottom of the stairs, still in his dressing gown and holding his half-drunk cup of coffee. When they reached the mansion, Artie was already there, staring at it - deep in thought. Within a minute, they had all scaled the large apple tree, dropped into the wild garden and pushed open the heavy front door.

Everything inside was just as they had left it.

They sprinted across the hallway, up the grand staircase without looking at any of the pictures on the wall and along the modest hallway to the undersized door. Kat reached out and began to turn the handle.

She expected it, for some reason, to resist her - to say, this time - you cannot come in; but the door opened just as easily as it had before.

Her jaw dropped. There was no machine.

The room was completely empty. There was no green flowing through the floors, no incredible polished and blackened contraption, no brother to the sister that brought them home - no way back to Fabrakka.

'I don't…' blurted out Kat. 'How…?'

Lewis held his sister as the words tumbled out of her, making less and less sense as they came.

Artie turned in a full circle, looking all around the room, trying to figure something out. Then he spoke.

'The connection between these worlds is a kind of puzzle. We need to find the solution - the key to unlock it, that will allow us to travel back there again. The answers are all in here, somewhere, and together we will find them, and we will crack it. If it takes days, weeks or months - we will solve this mystery.'

'There are pictures all over the walls of this house, pictures of people with information, answers and - I'll bet - deep, deep secrets. We will find out who they are, and what they know about Professor Alexander and all of his work.'

Lewis nodded his head frantically in agreement. He looked at his sister and his best friend and in that instant realised how much they had all grown in less than one day.

'Fabrakka was stuck, and we freed it,' he said confidently.

'Fabrakka was helpless, and we came to its aid,' said Kat.

'Fabrakka may now be in even greater danger, and the three of us - the Heroes of Fabrakka - will help it,' said Artie. 'I swear, here and now, that I will give everything I have to save that world and help our friends.'

He held out his right hand in front of himself. Lewis put his right hand on top of Artie's.

'I swear. Everything I have,' he said.

Kat thrust out her right hand. 'I swear too. Everything I have.'

'Heroes of Fabrakka - the Pact is made,' said Artie, his grin widening.

As she realised that their adventures in Fabrakka were only just beginning, Kat's hazelnut eyes blazed and sparkled with green.

EPILOGUE

The snow continued to fall heavily, blanketing every visible surface with pure sparkling white and forming large drifts against every upright. The old blackened machine turned its head towards the sky, longing for past times when days like these were impossible. Its processor was not what it once was, and it struggled to remember how long the snow had been falling.

It resumed its journey towards the great doors that loomed ahead, slowly dragging the heavy coffin-like caskets behind which made perfectly straight tracks in the snow. However deep they were, they were still not deep enough to reveal the oily black surface infused with the shimmering silver charge, whose power struggled to fully radiate upwards through the thick, ever-present snow.

The machine reached the doors to the great hall and the usual dance of secret knock, access code, deep scan, identity confirmation and reluctant admittance played out. The machine hated that these things had infiltrated its world and become part of its everyday language.

It began to cross the great hall, whose collapsed roof had allowed as much snow to form inside as out. The machine was unsteady in the snow - its right leg was incomplete and where there should have been a stabilising foot there was only a fractured limb spilling wires that slithered across the snow as it dragged its bulky frame another step. As it passed the huge and imposing statue, the machine glanced disapprovingly at it - disgusted that it even existed. It stopped at the base of the throne and gently laid down its cargo.

'Well?' asked the King as it raised its colossal frame from the seat. 'Are you sure?'

The machine turned and waved its right appendage over the left casket. The seamless surface of the casket revealed joins as if from nowhere, and quickly disintegrated. The cracked lens of the machine stuttered and refocused, scanning the features of the item within - calculating the distances between various points and matching it to its ancient records. Feelings it had not had in hundreds of cycles flooded its insides as it studied the unconscious child's dark red-flecked hair and lightly freckled face.

'I am sure,' replied Eight.

COPYRIGHT

ISBN: 9798435860818